FIELD OF ENDEAVOUR AND DEATH

Fergus P Egan

FIELD OF ENDEAVOUR AND DEATH

Author and Publisher: Fergus P Egan

ISBN: 978-1-7776037-2-4 (Paperback Edition)

ISBN: 978-1-7776037-3-1 (Hardcover Edition)

ISBN: 978-1-7776037-4-8 (Electronic Book Edition)

Email: FergusEganPublishing@gmail.com

Editor: Andrew Niall Egan
Cover Photos: Fergus P Egan

Disclaimer

This book is a work of fiction. For authenticity, iconic streets and buildings are accurately identified. Any resemblance to actual persons or events is entirely coincidental.

ISBN: 978-1-7776037-2-4

Sergei Falkov is sent to the United States of America to promote Russian trade. Following the death of Lenin, he is recalled to Russia. Russia has undergone significant changes in his absence. Under Stalin's repressive rule, he is sentenced to a forced-labour camp to purge him of capitalist contamination. Sergei experiences harsh conditions in the camp. He struggles to endure the process of rehabilitation. Lacking the strength of the younger fellow prisoners, he relies instead on cunning to survive.

FIELD OF ENDEAVOUR AND DEATH
LIST OF CHIEF CHARACTERS

Sergei Murashko Falkov
inventor and innovator

Dmitry Reshetnikov
senior civil servant,
Ministry of Labour and Social Protection

Ivan Patrushev
official in Ministry of the Interior,
Corrective Labour Camps Division

Denis Novak
administrator of a labour camp

Vladimir Kotyakov
manager of a corrective labour farm

Pyotr, Gregori, Boris, Mikhail
farmworkers

Olga Abramchenko
manager of a collective farm

Alexander Matytsin
inspector, Corrective Labour Camps

FIELD OF ENDEAVOUR AND DEATH

Fergus P Egan

CHAPTER ONE

Russia To America

"Comrade Falkov, please take a seat."

Sergei Murashko Falkov obeys the request – it is a command. He is visibly nervous. But his excitement far outweighs his feeling of apprehension. Sergei, recently turned 49, knows that if this visit were mere trouble then he would be in the presence of a much lower official. No, this is undoubtedly an honour, though perhaps also with an element of peril. Any visit with a senior official is fraught with danger. Sergei was prudent in his choice of attire. He has dressed appropriately in a European-style suit after the fashion favoured by Comrade Lenin. His beard is neatly trimmed. He coughs to settle himself and looks across the desk at Dmitry Reshetnikov. Dmitry is similarly attired. Sergei notes the absence of rank displayed on the official's clothing. Yet, authority exudes from every movement and gesture. Comrade Dmitry Reshetnikov is a senior official in the Civil Service of Sovnarkom (Sovet Narodnykh Komissarov – Council of People's Commissars), the government of the Soviet republic. The Soviet official opens a desk drawer and removes a cigarette box. He invites Sergei to choose a cigarette. The nervous guest declines and regards the official's stare with trepidation. Dmitry Reshetnikov blinks only when speaking. Otherwise, he stares with stone-grey eyes. He selects a cigarette, lights it and places the box back into the desk drawer. The exhaled smoke drifts up past the framed picture of Vladimir Lenin. Sergei feels the cold eyes of both men peering down at him. He coughs again and glances around. The office is bare of any other furniture or decoration. Even the ashtray is out of sight, concealed within the partly-open desk drawer. A sole file folder occupies the centre of the desktop. He glances quickly at the lone file and returns his gaze to the unblinking eyes.

"Comrade Falkov, do you know why you are here?"

Sergei is taken aback by the unexpected question. "I don't know. I was brought here."

"You were brought here against your will?"

"No, no… I mean that nothing was explained to me. And I was not expecting…"

"But tell me, why do you think you are here?" Dmitry blinks at the word 'think' and resumes his steady stare.

Sergei is reluctant to give his opinion. Should he say the wrong thing, it could be to his detriment. He plays it safe by tendering a non-committal response. "It is my service to Mother Russia. We are all servants of our glorious motherland."

"Quite so." Dmitry opens the file folder and glances at the top sheet of paper. It contains the letterhead of Sovnarkom and multiple ink-stamps. He continues, "I see that your service to Russia is admirable. But we consider that another field of endeavour would be of greater service."

"In another field, Comrade Reshetnikov?" Sergei experiences heightened excitement matched by an equally heightened feeling of unease.

"You are an inventor, are you not?"

"Yes. You may be familiar with the 'To/Fro Balanced Hinge' that…"

"I have knowledge of that. And of some thirty other inventions." He taps his finger on the stack of papers in the folder. "And you travel throughout Russia promoting these inventions and their benefits."

"Not all Russia. I travel to major towns accessible by rail…"

" …on a rail pass provided free to you." Dmitry pauses to let this piece of knowledge sink in. In a society where all are regarded as equal, such a privilege is unusual. This is a reminder to Sergei that he is indebted to Russia for this rare favour. Dmitry blinks and resumes speaking. "Your inventions are beneficial? Yes, I agree."

Sergei exhales in relief. He realizes that he had been holding his breath, not knowing where the conversation was leading. He shifts his feet and relaxes in the chair. He wonders if he should respond, but decides that it could be considered a rude interruption.

"But that is not all you do. Inventing. No?" Dmitry slowly swivels his chair until he is in profile. He leans his head back against the chair and stares lazily at the ceiling. He softly repeats his remark. "But that is not all you do, is it?"

Sergei fears that the conversation is taking an ominous turn. "Well, yes. I also work as an interpreter…"

"…in the Ministry of Communications. Yes, I know. What do you interpret there?"

"I translate foreign news reports into Russian. And I translate Russian press releases into English for our English Language Services."

"So you are fluent in English?" Dmitry Reshetnikov poses the question in English with no hint of a Russian accent.

This time, Sergei is unable to hide his surprise. He rises to his feet. For a moment, he is unable to respond. Dmitry appears to have fallen asleep, except that he moves his cigarette to his lips. He takes a slow drag and awaits an answer. Sergei recovers and resumes his seat. "Yes, Comrade Reshetnikov," he addresses the official in English, "I am fluent in written and spoken English."

Dmitry Reshetnikov swivels his chair back to face the surprised Sergei. He removes a sealed envelope from the file folder and slides it towards the unsettled inventor-interpreter. "You are going to America. Here are your instructions."

From this point on, the entire conversation is rendered in English. Sergei Falkov raises his voice, much louder than he intended. "America? Why am I going to America?"

"To sell Russian inventions to the Americans. Not just your own inventions, but those on the list we give you. You will ensure that these inventions are patented in the United States; you will convince American manufacturers and businesses to adopt them; you will ensure that the resulting royalties are lodged into appropriate bank accounts for the benefit and use of

Soviet Russia."

"Can this be done? I mean, we don't have diplomatic relations with the U.S."

"You are correct in stating that we do not enjoy diplomatic relations with a country that refuses to formally recognize our Soviet government. But don't you read the communiques and news reports that go through the Ministry of Communications? Since the end of last year, we have developed trade and economic ties with the United States of America. You will go there. While there, you will work through our trade mission office in Washington." Dmitry shifts back to the official language and asks in Russian, "Are you clear?"

Sergei performs a quick memory search. He is knowledgeable of Soviet policies. In 1920, the government brought in universal labour conscription ensuring that all citizens between the ages of 16 and 50 had to work. In the same year, Lenin sought to advance the Russian economy through foreign trade. The significance of his mission is clear. In his new service to Russia, 49-year-old Sergei Falkov is mandated to contribute to the economy through foreign trade. To purchase foreign goods, Russia requires hard currency like the U.S. dollar. And Sergei's new job is to collect

U.S. dollars to help finance Russia's foreign purchases. He responds to Dmitry's parting question. "I understand. When do I leave? And what will be my duration in America?"

"You will be informed of your departure details. In due course, we will let you know when to return home. Read your instructions. It's all in there – all you need to know for now. Carry out the orders and be prepared to leave at a moment's notice."

Clearly the meeting is over. Dmitry gestures to the door. Sergei departs.

Over the next two weeks, Sergei makes the necessary preparations. On 10 June 1923, he boards a freighter in Leningrad, bound for New York. Plans, blueprints and prototype models of Russian inventions are safely stored aboard. As the ship pulls away from the pier, he is looking forward to living and working in America. And it is financed by an expense account at his disposal. In his excitement, he punches the air. "As they say in America," he exclaims in English, "Jackpot!"

CHAPTER TWO

HOME IN THE USSR

"Comrade Falkov, you will remain standing."

Sergei Murashko Falkov obeys. He is visibly nervous. Dmitry Reshetnikov's office has changed little in five years. But Russia has undergone a considerable transformation since Joseph Stalin became the leader of Soviet Russia in January 1924. Comrade Dmitry Reshetnikov retains his senior position in the Civil Service of Sovnarkom. This is obvious. Sergei immediately assesses the small, but significant, changes in the official's office. The absence of a tobacco smell is striking. Dmitry no longer smokes, or at least not in his office. Instead, there is a lingering smell of vodka. Sergei suppresses a smile. Vodka is said to be odourless. But this is not so. It is a myth that consumers of vodka believe. Vodka drinkers are oblivious of the vaporous smell of the spirit in the same way as a fish is unaware of the water in which it swims. But it is quite noticeable to anyone on the outside – both the vodka smell and the water. Where a picture of Lenin once adorned the wall, the space is currently graced with a picture of a smiling Stalin. Dmitry, seated below, is dressed in what could be mistaken for a military officer's uniform. However, it is not an officer's uniform since it displays no rank. Rather, it is military-style clothing emulating the attire of the respected Soviet leader. And Dmitry's hairline has receded perceptibly. There is one additional piece of furniture. A small stand against a wall contains a bust of Lenin. The sculpture is polished black and is adorned with a fresh red carnation placed in front. How strange it is that a professed atheist reveres the image of the deceased Lenin in such a manner. It is like a shrine to a saint.

Sergei Falkov has also undergone a change in five years. Today, standing before the officious Dmitry Reshetnikov, he is dressed in an American lightweight suit – somewhat creased from his recent travel. The colour is light grey, much favoured in American business circles. Whereas he was previously full-bearded, Sergei now sports a stylish goatee. And his hair has receded in step with his reduced facial hair – you lose a little; you lose a lot. He also wears glasses now. In America, he was considered to be a 'dashing Russian', always appropriately attired for a business meeting. Today, standing before the critical eye of the Sovnarkom official, Sergei realizes that, here in Moscow, his appearance in American clothing is considered foreign and improper.

The most significant changes that occurred in Russia since Sergei's departure in 1923 are quite drastic. After the death of Vladimir Lenin, Joseph Stalin became the leader of Soviet Russia in January 1924. Stalin's understanding of communism differs markedly from Lenin's. And by 1928 the new leader had dismantled Lenin's economic policies and had implemented a campaign to reform Soviet agriculture and industry. He destroyed prosperous peasant farmers and instituted collectivization of agriculture. Private ownership of the land was prohibited. This remains in effect to this day. As a result, much of what is produced is surrendered to the government. Vast territorial expansion occurred that rivalled the previous Czarist empire. The Russian Soviet Republic became the Russian Soviet Federative Socialist Republic, albeit it is simply referred to as Russia (or Soviet Russia or the Russian Federation). Furthermore, the Union of Soviet Socialist Republics (the Soviet Union or USSR) was formed, governed by the Communist Party of the Soviet Union with Moscow as its capital. Within the USSR today, the Russian SFSR is the most populous of the Soviet republics. The USSR stretches from Ukrainian SSR and Byelorussian SSR in the west to the Siberian Pacific coast. The ambitious Stalin also looked westwards. But westward expansion is currently blocked by the presence of German interests. However, he took advantage of the 1922 agreement with the German Republic, an agreement in contravention of the Versailles Treaty, to increase trade with Germany. His hidden agenda is to strengthen the Communist Party in Germany hoping that, in time, it will lead to the collapse of the capitalist nation and open the way to USSR western expansion.

Today, 25 August 1928, Sergei Murashko Falkov is home. Standing before this stern civil servant official, Dmitry Reshetnikov, Sergei wonders if he can ever be truly at home in Stalin's new Russia.

"Comrade Falkov, do you know why you are here?"

"I was summoned here."

"And why, do you think, you were summoned here?"

Sergei fears that the wrong answer could land him in trouble. Worse, the correct answer could be more disastrous. He responds, "To be of service, Comrade Reshetnikov."

Dmitry clicks his tongue in thought. He blinks and speaks again. "You wish to be of service? Doing what?" He taps the file folder on his desk. "Your previous assignment did not go well. Is that not so, Comrade Falkov?"

Sergei swallows. The meeting is going from bad to worse. "It did at first, Comrade Reshetnikov. But the Americans acted unfairly – fraudulently actually." He hopes that by blaming the Americans he can shift blame to where he believes it truly belongs.

"And you let them. Are you saying that you were manipulated by capitalist entrepreneurs? And that you failed to outsmart them?"

Sergei fears that he might be subjected to some of Stalin's extreme forms of justice with its reported instruments of extrajudicial punishment. He weakly pleads his case. "At first, in the first year, the patented products and inventions were warmly received. But later, the crooked Americans copied them and made sufficient minor modifications to qualify as alternative patents. The Americans duly registered them and promoted them. The American patents were promoted and favoured over ours."

"And our royalty receipts decreased as a result."

"Americans are capricious, impulsive and fickle-minded. What is popular today is disregarded tomorrow. That is why a good marketing strategy is important. Old products and ideas need to be presented as new, over and over again. It could just be as simple as changing the packaging or just a fresh sales pitch."

"So, did your marketing strategy work?"

"It was on course…"

"It was on course and costly. While the revenues dropped, your expenses rose."

Sergei opens his mouth to speak. But thinks better of it and remains silent. What could he say other than admit to being negligent in promoting the Russian patents in the face of the inferior American counterfeits?

"Comrade Falkov, you will be taken to the flat we have prepared for you. It is one of the apartments provided for Kremlin officials. While there, you will prepare a detailed report of your time in America. There is a typewriter available in your flat. Use it. I wish to receive your completed report in two days. And remember, the report is to include everything you did in America – your work, your play, your friendships, your business contacts, all which is savoury and unsavoury – during your five-year stint there."

Sergei is relieved to hear this. He is being sent to a comfortable flat, not a prison. Undoubtedly, he will be reprimanded or punished in some way as a consequence of the perceived failure of his assignment in the United States of America. It appears that Dmitri accepts that U.S. capitalism stymied the venture through American underhand trickery. If the humiliated inventor is not fully absolved, surely this explanation greatly lessens his culpability. Sergei vows to himself to highlight American corruption in his pending report.

Having spoken, Dmitri places the file folder inside a desk drawer and shouts to an attendant to enter the office. "Comrade Saveliev!"

Saveliev immediately enters. He must have been standing by the door in expectation of the summons. "Yes, Comrade Reshetnikov!"

"Take Comrade Falkov to his flat."

"Yes, Comrade."

Sergei is relieved to be leaving the presence of Dmitry Reshetnikov. He is worried about his future and what new duties will be entrusted to him – or imposed upon him. As the two men exit, Dmitri expresses a parting remark. "Comrade Falkov, I trust you like potatoes."

CHAPTER THREE

LIVING IN THE USSR

Ulitsa Bol'shaya Lubyanka is a street within 15 minutes' walking distance of Red Square and the Kremlin if one walks via Mokhovaya Street. Sergei Falkov knows this from his earlier visits to the GUM department store. Of course, that was before Stalin converted the GUM into office space for his Five-Year Plan. Sergei's escort, Saveliev, brings him to an impressive building. Before the Revolution, this edifice would have been regarded as affluent. But today the previously opulent apartments are divided into one-room and two-room flats. Upon entering through the front door, they are confronted by the portye (doorman) who appears to be expecting them.

"This must be Comrade Falkov. We are prepared for you. Your flat is ready. Ascend the stairs to the attic, room 4. I trust you find it adequate to your needs."

The portye expects Sergei to find his way, unaided, to attic flat 4. Saveliev, having fulfilled his duty, departs without a word. Sergei walks along an elaborate corridor until he encounters a splendid staircase. He ascends the marble steps to the first floor, to the second floor, to the third floor. At each level, the staircase is less ornate. The stairs to the fifth floor are narrow and simply carpeted. The stair runner is held in place by brass rods at each step. At last, he reaches the staircase to the attic. The narrow wooden stairs are humble, uncarpeted and unpainted. They are also quite steep. Upon reaching the attic, he realizes that this was once the servants' sleeping quarters. He proceeds along the landing to a door marked by a large '4'. He turns the door handle – the door is unlocked – and enters the flat.

It is strange to enter new accommodation without a suitcase. Sergei carries nothing except the clothes he is wearing and the contents of his pockets. It is a one-room spartan flat with a window. He peers around. The bed against the wall serves as a couch. Or does the couch serve as a bed? There is a desk and chair next to the second wall, the wall with the window. He notes the typewriter and paper neatly positioned on the desk. There is a counter built into another wall. It contains a gas cooker with two burners, enough to boil a kettle and heat a pot. There is a cupboard at the end of the counter. The fourth wall, the one with the door, has a small stand containing the bust of Lenin. This is similar to the bust he observed in Dmitry Reshetnikov's office.

The tired Sergei removes his jacket and hangs it on the hook on the door. The tension he experienced in his encounter with Dmitry Reshetnikov is easing. He longs to rest, even sleep. Suddenly, he is unexpectedly interrupted by a knock at the door and a woman's voice.

"Comrade Falkov?"

He wonders who it could be. He responds, "Yes. Who is it?"

"The building ekonomka." It is a visit by the housekeeper.

The door opens. He beholds a stern-faced woman. She is 60ish with a pale face; greying hair pulled back into a bun; dark-grey jacket with black epaulets over a matching skirt displaying large deep pockets; black stockings; black low-heeled shoes; 160cms from heel to hair bun. She is holding a steaming cup in her left hand. He bids her enter, whereupon she tenders him a mug of hot tea. Sergei graciously accepts the welcoming tea. The ekonomka casts a critical eye around the flat and pauses upon seeing the jacket hanging at the back of the door. Sergei is unable to read her poker face. He cannot tell if she disapproves of the foreign-looking clothing, or if she is merely curious. Skipping any small talk, the ekonomka rhymes off the rules for staying in the building. Sergei attempts to memorize them:

- There is no key to the flat. Why would one need to lock the door in a secure building? There is a locking button on the inside door handle that prevents entry from the landing, except for the ekonomka who has a device like a knitting needle that can pop the release.

- There is no running water on the attic level. The shared bathroom is on the fourth floor. There is a communal kitchen next to the bathroom for use by occupants of the attic level.

- It is permitted to make tea and heat soup in the flat, but not to cook anything smoky or smelly – so don't fry fish.

- Bed linens are changed weekly.

- Laundry service is available.

- All housekeeping services are at the standard rate set by the government.

Sergei fears that the list of rules outweighs his ability to remember them all. No doubt, the ekonomka will set him straight if he blunders. There appears to be no prohibition on drinking and smoking as evidenced by the numerous ring marks and cigarette burns on the counter. Having delivered her standard welcome address, the practical matron departs.

Sergei drains the remaining tea from the mug, sets it down on the counter and collapses onto the bed in relief. He immediately jumps back up to his feet. He realizes that he has no food in the flat. And that he has no change of clothing. He has worn his undergarments continuously for a week; his sole suit is wrinkled. His priority, before sleep, is to obtain food and clothing. He checks his wallet. He is satisfied that he has sufficient roubles for his purchases, the proceeds of the U.S. dollars he exchanged in Leningrad upon re-entering Russia.

Sergei attempts to exit the building but he is prevented by the portye. "Comrade Falkov, you are to remain in the building, in your flat or in the common areas."

Sergei is taken aback. "Why? I need to make some urgent purchases. Surely I may leave for a short period."

"The ministry wants you to remain available at a moment's notice."

"The ministry? What ministry?"

"I don't know which ministry. There are so many ministries. It is the ministry you work for, is it not?"

Sergei is momentarily confused. Why would the

Ministry of Communications require him to stand by? Perhaps he is to be reassigned back to his old job as an interpreter. Sergei prepares to plead with the portye but is interrupted by the arrival of a senior military officer who enters the building carrying an attaché case and a red carnation. The officer nods in recognition to the portye and raises his eyebrows at Sergei's inappropriate American garb. He walks into the interior of the building. Sergei lowers his voice and explains his predicament to the officious doorman.

"Comrade Portye, I arrived here today. I did not have time to pack my things or make preparations before my arrival. I need to eat some food and obtain a change of clothing. It is important."

"Comrade Falkov, I am sorry. But you are to remain here until you are summoned. However, if you require food, arrange it with the ekonomka. She might also be able to provide you with some clothing. Her unit is on the ground floor at the back of the building. Go see her."

Sergei hurries off to the ekonomka. He is interrupted en route by the military officer.

"Comrade Falkov? Did I hear correctly? I couldn't help but overhear your conversation back there," pointing in the direction of the doorman. "But are you not Sergei Falkov, the renowned Russian inventor?"

Sergei is taken aback by this sudden and unexpected question. He responds cautiously, "I am Sergei Falkov. And I am an inventor, yes. But renowned? That is a matter of opinion."

"Come now. I remember you some years ago when you visited Omsk. That was…"

"Six years ago."

"And here you are in Moscow. Why are you dressed like an American? Oh, I'm Ivan Patrushev. In here you can call me 'Ivan'. Out there," pointing to an imaginary distant spot, "I am Colonel Patrushev."

Sergei relaxes. This colonel appears to be friendly. Perhaps he can help. "Please call me 'Sergei'. I am pleased to meet you, Ivan. And why am I dressed like an American? Well, I have just returned from the U.S. where I was working with the Russian Trade Mission in Washington. I'm afraid I was summoned back unexpectedly and did not have time to pack a change of clothes."

"And this is how a Russian dresses in America? A suit like this? And an American shirt…"

"The shirt is Italian."

"And American shoes…"

"The shoes are English oxfords. But this is not the customary dress code for the Russian staff in the Russian Trade Mission." Sergei laughs. "No, this is my attire for business meetings with Americans. However, I fear it is inappropriate here in Moscow."

"I see. And you didn't have an opportunity to change. Well, that's quite common – being summoned unexpectedly with no time to prepare. I suffered that fate once. Ever since then, I live out of a suitcase – always prepared."

"So, you work at the Kremlin?"

"Yes. Everyone here does."

"What do you do?"

Ivan responds in a gruff voice. "No one asks about the work in the Kremlin."

Sergei shivers and holds his breath. Ivan slaps him hard, but jovially, on the shoulder. The slap knocks the breath out of him. He manages a feeble laugh.

Ivan resumes in a friendly voice. "Your predicament,

Sergei, not the Kremlin, is my priority now. Come, let's go see the warden ekonomka. She is really a warm-hearted babushka behind the stern exterior."

Ivan is true to his word. He escorts Sergei to the housekeeping unit and speaks briefly with the ekonomka. He succinctly describes Sergei's dilemma. Thereupon, he rushes off to the Kremlin. He shouts back as he walks away, "I finish work at seven. I'll drop by to see how you are coping when I return."

The ekonomka is not one for idle chatter. She frowns at her new tenant and asks, "Do you like potatoes?"

To be polite, he responds, "Potatoes? Yes, of course."

"Good. Go to your flat." With that, she pushes him gently out of the unit and shuts the door.

Sergei is more tired than before. It is an effort to climb the five flights of stairs. He enters the flat and stumbles to the bed. He lands heavily and invites sleep. Unfortunately, he is disturbed by knocking at the door – not the sound of knuckles rapping, but the sound of someone kicking the door. Annoyed, Sergei opens the door. The babushka ekonomka enters with both hands laden. She goes immediately to the counter to unburden her load.

"Here, Comrade Falkov," she says. "This is a bowl of potato soup. Eat it while it is warm. And here is a pot of borscht you can heat up later. There are matches for the gas in the drawer below with all the spoons and stuff." With that, she leaves before the surprised tenant can thank her.

Sergei quickly downs the warm welcoming broth. Once again, he flops down onto the bed. This time the urge to sleep is overpowering. When next he hears a knock at the door, he remains lying face down and mutters in a muffled voice, "Enter." He is vaguely aware of the ekonomka speaking about unclaimed laundry from previous tenants. And he falls to sleep.

Later, Dmitry awakens. It is still light. He is unsure of the time. There is no point in searching for the watch in his pocket. He has not wound it in over a day. He decides to look at it anyway. But he is unable to locate his jacket pocket. He fully awakens and realizes that he is covered by a blanket; his jacket is hanging on the door hook; his shoes are missing from his feet. He jumps out of bed and almost steps on them. He has no recollection of removing his jacket and shoes. He rubs his eyes and looks for other surprises. There is a fresh red carnation placed at Lenin's bust. He discovers his biggest surprise in the drawer of the cupboard – neatly folded underwear, socks and shirts. "The ekonomka!"

he exclaims aloud. "Ivan is correct about her being a warm-hearted babushka."

Now that he is somewhat refreshed from his nap, Sergei realizes that he has not bathed in almost a week. He feels dirty. So, choosing items from among the laundered clothes, he goes down to the bathroom. After a tepid bath, he shaves and trims his goatee. He feels clean in fresh underwear. But he still contends with the wrinkled suit. Back in the flat, he wonders where to place his dirty underwear. There must be a procedure for sending it for laundering, but he is unable to recollect what instructions the ekonomka told him. He sits on the bed and looks disdainfully at the typewriter on the desk. He is required to complete a comprehensive report of his time in the United States. He seeks an excuse to postpone the annoying but obligatory task. His wish is granted. He is alerted by a sharp knocking at his door.

"Sergei! It's Ivan! Are you in?"

Before he answers, Ivan opens the door and bursts in. He presents a bottle of vodka, which he places on the desk, and then he also slaps down a pack of cigarettes. Strangely, he carries an army uniform folded over his left arm. He turns to face Sergei, who sits with mouth agape, and says, "Hey, you didn't forget, did you? I told you I would come."

"Yes… No…I mean, of course, I didn't forget. What time is it?"

"It is half-past seven. And guess what?"

Before he responds, he is aware that Ivan did not come alone. The ekonomka also enters the room. She looks critically at the pot of borscht. "You haven't eaten?"

"No. I fell asleep."

Things begin to happen. Sergei feels that he is being swept up in a busy game. The ekonomka heats the borscht. Ivan describes how he found the army uniform when he first moved into his flat, left behind by a soldier who departed in a hurry. This appears to be a common issue. But here now, in Sergei's flat, he and the housekeeper attend to the uniform and remove the collar marks and chevrons. They decide to leave the buttons intact. They dress Sergei in the uniform. It is almost to his size, but a little large. The housekeeper sticks pins in various places and directs him to remove the jacket and trousers carefully. She remarks aloud to herself, "Just a few adjustments and I'll have Comrade Falkov looking like a Russian again."

Sergei is greatly taken by the woman's kindness.

"Comrade Ekonomka, how can I repay you?"

"There is no charge for this. It does not come under the approved duties that are subject to a fee. And you know that I am prohibited from profiting from a tenant. However, I can do you another favour which benefits us both. I'll take the American suit that you shouldn't wear in Russia. I can make something out of it."

This is agreeable to Sergei. The ekonomka departs from the flat, taking the suit and the dirty underwear for laundering. Ivan laughs at Sergei who is now dressed exclusively in his underwear and will remain so until the alterations are executed on his new-found Russian clothing. Sergei joins in the laughter. Then they dine together on borscht and share the vodka. Sergei declines to smoke, but Ivan puffs like a chimney. They utilize the desk as a table and, since there is but one chair, they drag the bed up close.

Ivan is curious about America. He poses many questions. Sergei explains that he is required to complete a comprehensive account of his time in the United States. He begins to relate his story and types as he proceeds.

Ivan continues to ask probing questions. "Is everyone rich in America?"

"No, just a few. Most people are far from rich but they dream of attaining wealth."

"Are they better off than us Russians here?"

"Better? Some things are better there; some things are not so. There is the good and the bad. In my experience, there is more bad than good in America."

"So, what is the bad?"

"The rich steal from the poor. They call it 'profit'. It is legal and encouraged. However, if the poor steal, it is a punishable offence."

"The exploitation of the working class? Yes?"

"That's how Marx referred to it in 'Das Kapital', the Communist Manifesto. But Marx did not fully appreciate the American political economy of 75 years later."

"Sergei, it is dangerous to criticize Marx."

"Criticize Marx? No. Extrapolate his theories into 20th-century America. The rich exploit the poor, yes. But they also exploit each other in fierce competition to achieve a controlling monopoly. They cheat; they break their words; they defraud and embezzle to gain the upper hand. And all this is fuelled by greed."

"Americans are greedy and untrustworthy in the name of profit at any cost?"

"No. Not all Americans. Just the few who attempt to wield control over the economy – politicians, entrepreneurs and business tycoons."

"You say that there is the good as well as the bad. So, what did you find good?"

"*Nightclubs,*" Sergei renders in English.

"*Nightclubs? What are nightclubs?*"

"Places of *'wine, women and song'.*" Sergei then explains it in Russian. "Places of drink, women and frivolity. There is a ban on the sale of alcoholic beverages in America. Yet many nightclubs operate unimpeded – apparently the rich have ways of circumventing the laws. I conducted many meetings in these places. I concluded deals with capitalists for the benefit of Russia. I once had an agreement with 'Ford Motor Company'. Unfortunately, all these deals fell through. Some were short-lived; others never materialized. In the end, after five years of work… Well."

"Surely, in all these dealings, you made some friends?"

"Friends?" Sergei searches his memory and smiles faintly. "For a while, I believed so. I had an 'affair of the heart' with a woman named Anne Brennan. She was, still is, the wife of Senator James Brennan. But she manipulated me into a doomed deal just to give the appearance of a possible economic venture in her husband's state. He used this to garner votes. Once he was elected, the deal fell apart. I was being used as a pawn."

"And you say that this was the good part?"

Sergei laughs and knocks back another shot of vodka. "No. Just the *nightclubs.*"

"Ah, 'drink, women and frivolity' met with your approval, but not the deal-making."

"In a nutshell, yes."

On the following day, Sergei completes his report. The ekonomka brings him his well-fitting new clothing. The portye arranges for the report to be picked up. The ekonomka continues to bring him tea, potato broth and borscht every day. Sergei remains confined to the building awaiting his new assignment.

CHAPTER FOUR

Hammer and Sickle

Sergei Falkov is alerted by the sound of feet entering the flat. He looks up from his desk at the two soldiers now standing before him. He addresses them as he struggles to formulate a sentence. "Comrades, are you here…?"

The senior soldier interrupts him with a directive. It is rendered straightforwardly, neither as a threat nor a blandishment. "Comrade Falkov, you are to accompany us. You are to leave at once."

Sergei is surprised by the urgent summons. But then again, he had been forewarned to be ready at a moment's notice. He rises from his chair and warily approaches the two soldiers. He points to his tunic hanging behind the door. He asks, "My tunic? I'll need my tunic."

"Of course. Don your tunic." The soldier glances at Sergei's feet and at his English shoes. "And fasten your shoelaces."

Sergei, having recovered somewhat from his surprise, deduces that he is being brought to his new assignment. But surely he could have found his way to the ministry unaided. Thereupon he realizes that he is unsure of which ministry he is to report to and to which address. When he is ready, he pats his tunic smooth and says agreeably, "All right. Let's be on our way."

They travel by car to their destination. Neither soldier gives any clue on where they are going. Wherever it is, it is in a part of Moscow unfamiliar to Sergei. They stop before a massive brick building. There is no signage to indicate the purpose of the building. Sergei assumes that it is a Czarist-era warehouse building converted into offices by the Sovnarkom, just as the GUM in Red Square is transformed into offices. Sergei is escorted through the front doors, down a short corridor and into a room. Suddenly, he is filled with dread by the tense atmosphere he senses. He is confronted by two stern-faced men in uniform.

The older (higher ranking?) man speaks curtly. "Comrade Falkov, remove your clothing!"

Confused by the command, Sergei attempts to ask for clarification. "Remove my…?"

'Slap!' An unexpected swift slap to his face unbalances Sergei for a moment. The man barks at him. "When I give an order, do it!"

Sergei grasps that this is not a job interview. He is

under arrest. Fearful of any further calamitous consequences, he quickly removes his clothing and stands trembling before the man in his underwear.

'Slap!'

The second slap land with more force. He falls to one knee. But the message is clear. He removes all his clothing until he is completely naked. Man number two takes the bundle of clothes and examines the items. Man number one, meantime, examines Sergei's body. He prods every area. He sticks his finger into the frightened man's mouth. He has Sergei bend over and part his buttocks. When satisfied, he orders the prisoner to stand erect. Man number two returns his clothes to him and orders him to dress. At this point, Sergei learns that the belts are missing from his trousers and tunic, all the buttons have been removed and the laces are gone from his shoes. The guards, for this is what they must be, march the prisoner down a brightly-lit corridor to another room. Sergei stumbles along between them. He holds his trousers in place with one hand and grips his shirt and tunic closed with the other hand. He drags his heels as he flops awkwardly in his English shoes. The second room is marked 'Holding Cell'. They thrust Sergei inside and shut the metal door with a resounding clang.

The holding cell is five metres by six. It is windowless but is brightly lit by GOELRO, the State Commission for Electrification of Russia. There is a grating in the centre of the floor for drainage. Sharp spikes protrude from all the walls. Twenty inmates stand around, some leaning against each other. A guard shouts, "Remain standing! Do not sit or lie on the floor. Sleep is prohibited. Talking is prohibited. You will suffer severe punishment if you disobey. Should you refuse to adhere to the rules, you will be shot. You will remain here until summoned."

Sergei chokes on the foul odours of the cell. He coughs. His eyes water. After a few seconds, he dares to breathe. He looks around for a free space in which to stand. His feet slip as he shuffles. The floor is wet and slick from urine and feces. Throughout the following hours, Sergei learns that the rules are enforced differently depending on the status of the inmate. Three of the prisoners are bullies. These are murderers and thugs. Because they are followers of the Revolution, they are treated more favourably than others. The remaining inmates are dissidents of one kind or another – regarded as subversive to the communist order. Once a day, the guards throw bread into the cell to feed the detainees. The three bullies claim the bread for themselves, leaving little or none for the others.

Likewise, a canister of drinking water is supplied. Some of the inmates endure an entire day without food or water or sleep. One other task, however, benefits them all equally. The detainees are marched out of the cell while worker-prisoners pour buckets of water onto the floor. Then they scrub the floor with yard brooms and push the fetid water into the drain in the centre of the floor.

Frequently, the guards enter and beat any prisoner who tries to rest on the ground. One inmate, weakened from the dire conditions, collapses to the floor. The guards hit him with batons. When he fails to stand up, they drag him to the door and shoot him in the head. The gunshot is deafening in the confined space. Another prisoner is subjected to verbal abuse by the bullies. They accuse him of anti-Soviet ideas just because he once taught political science. When he argues in defence, they throw him repeatedly against the spikes in the wall. The leader of the thugs grabs him by the hair and jams his head against a spike. The inmate is clearly dead when the brute hurls him to the ground. The guards enter and view the body. The thug tells them that he had slipped on the wet floor and smashed his head against the spikes in the wall. They accept the explanation and drag the dead body from the cell. Sergei witnesses this and fears for his safety. He stands stoically still, hoping that he can endure these intolerable conditions until he is summoned away from the holding cell – if he is ever summoned.

The chief bully approaches Sergei and asks him his name and his reason for being here. He considers lying but suspects that the brute already knows his name. As to why he is here, Sergei is not quite sure. So, he answers, "Sergei Falkov. And I am here because I ran afoul of vodka, women and frivolity."

The three bullies exchange looks. Then they laugh raucously. "Hah! A drunken jolly adulterer!"

This commotion draws the attention of the guards. One enters and hits Sergei in the small of the back with his baton. Sergei grimaces but remains standing. This intrusion by the guards causes the cell to fall quiet. Later, Sergei risks kneeling on one knee and rests his body against a fellow prisoner. And so he suffers through the first day. And into another day. He is unsure of the passage of time. He feels that he has been in the holding cell for days. He calculates the number of times the guards tossed bread into the cell. Twice. Therefore, this is the second day. At various times, detainees are called by name and are removed from the cell. They are replaced by new arrivals. One of the thugs is removed; the two remaining bullies are quiet. Sergei braves his way to the grating in the floor and avails of the drain hole. This is usually an opportunity for the thugs to abuse an inmate. However, on this occasion, no one kicks him while he is in a squatting position, or knocks him sprawling.

On day three, Sergei Falkov is summoned from the cell. The guards bring him to a room marked 'INTERROGATION' and seat him in a metal chair bolted to the floor. A prison guard stands beside him. A metal table is in front, three metres away, at which three men sit facing him. The electric light is angled to shine on Sergei's face and directed away from the three men. Their faces are hidden in shadow. One of the men addresses the prisoner.

"Comrade Sergei Murashko Falkov, you worked as an agent for a foreign hostile government. It will be easier for you if you sign a confession here and now."

Sergei is taken aback. He pleads his defence. "Comrades, I worked in the United States of America for five years, but exclusively on behalf of Soviet Russia." He has difficulty speaking. His tongue is dry and swollen from thirst. "There must be some mistake…"

The interrogator cuts him off. "We have your report

here..." he insists as he waves the report that Sergei compiled a few days earlier "...in which you describe how you revealed Soviet secrets to the Americans – industrial innovations and inventions. This makes you an American agent working against the interests of Soviet Russia."

Sergei could argue that this was precisely the purpose of his mission in America. It was an undertaking to amass hard currency for Russia's foreign trade. But he knows that this line of defence would work against him. He would then be accused of criticizing Russia's foreign policies. He hangs his head in defeat.

The interrogator continues, "Sign this confession." He holds a sheet of paper aloft, waves it pointedly at Sergei and gives it to a guard to bring to him.

Sergei blinks at the paper thrust in front of his face. Being weak from fatigue, he is unable to focus his eyes. The page is filled with blurred writing. He identifies the signature line at the bottom of the page, but not much else except for the heading, 'CONFESSION'. He remains limp with arms dangling at the sides.

Noting his hesitation, the interrogator whispers ominously, "If you need time to reflect on this, to delay your decision, we will return you to the holding cell for one more day. We can meet again tomorrow. In the meantime, it will be common knowledge that an American agent, a Russian traitor, is being held in custody – Sergei Murashko Falkov."

Sergei takes the pen from the guard and signs the proffered paper. Thus, he has confessed to the serious crime of sedition.

Sergei is taken from the interrogation room. The guard brings him to a washroom. There, he is made strip. The guard hoses him with cold water. The cold water shocks the weakened prisoner. He cups his hands and avails of the flowing water to drink the refreshing liquid. Afterwards, he is made to carry his bundle of clothes naked to a cell.

The new cell is different from the previous holding cell. It is small – three metres by two. A low bench is fixed into one wall – the bed – at the end of which is a higher small bench – the table. There is no window, but the cell is brightly illuminated by a single electric light. A waste bucket occupies the furthest corner. Sergei is relieved to see that it is a single-occupant cell, so no bully to share it with. The table contains a welcoming tin mug of water and a hunk of black bread. He immediately devours the bread and consumes the water. Next, he puts on his clothes and lies down on the rigid wood of the bed and falls to sleep.

Sergei is awakened by the sound of the cell door opening. He looks up from his bunk. He adjusts his glasses from where they had slipped down his nose and scrutinizes the visitor. At first he expects to see a guard but, instead, he recognizes Colonel Ivan Patrushev.

The colonel speaks. "Comrade Falkov, how are you holding up?"

Sergei swings his body to a sitting position on the edge of the bed. "Ivan?" he asks in surprise.

"Today, I am Colonel Patrushev." His voice has a touch of friendship, but the prisoner is in no doubt that this is an official visit. "I see that you have managed to retain your American glasses and your English shoes. But how are you?"

Sergei regards this as a pointless question. It is clear that his circumstances are awful. He answers by stating the obvious. "I am not dead. At least not yet. But I fear what may be in store for me."

The colonel approaches the bed and sits beside the inmate. "Comrade Falkov, I am well aware of your situation."

"How did you learn? And what do you know?"

"I have known for some time. And I was present at the interrogation earlier."

This is a shock for Sergei. Then again, why is he surprised at the machinations of the Sovnarkom and officials of the Politburo? He turns to look the colonel in the face and asks, "You were one of the three..?"

"…one of the three interrogators? Yes, I was." He pauses for a moment to measure the surprise displayed by Sergei. He continues. "Comrade, you are smart; you are stoic. I know this. Now listen carefully. You have a choice that will determine the rest of your life. The smart choice will benefit you in the long term; the alternative will ensure your death."

Sergei experiences a cold shiver. "Death? But, why?"

"While in America you were contaminated by their corrupt principles. That is why we called you back to Russia. Yes, your expenses increased as related revenues declined, but that was not the overriding reason for ordering your return. No, we called you back to realign you to Soviet Russia's communist ideologies. To be reinstated back into Russian society, you will undergo rehabilitation through labour." The colonel pauses for this to sink in. Then, he resumes. "Of course, this requires you to embrace your rehabilitation eagerly. Any hint of resistance or insincerity… Well, let's not consider the alternative scenario."

Sergei sighs. He asks weakly, "So, what should I do?"

"Tomorrow you will be sentenced. Before sentencing, you will be asked to make a statement. This is your opportunity to express contrition. Make reference to serving the state for the common good through labour. This is what we want to hear. You will be sentenced to serve in a corrective labour farm. The sentence will be open-ended, which means that you will be returned to society when you demonstrate rehabilitation. It is usually in excess of three years. It could be as long as eight years. Or it could be terminated suddenly if you step out of line. Problem workers are shot."

"What if I am not suitable for the work; if I am not physically strong enough?"

"Comrade Falkov, I have said it already – you are smart; you are stoic." With that, the colonel slaps him on the knee and rises from the bed. He shouts "Guard!" The cell door opens and he departs.

Sergei is left to his troubled thoughts. He surmises that

his present situation was predetermined and that Dmitry Reshetnikov and Colonel Patrushev knew all along and played him. Who else was part of the subterfuge? The building portye? The ekonomka? His thoughts are interrupted by the entrance of a prison guard bearing a metal tray. He places it on the table. It contains a bowl of steaming soup and a hunk of black bread. He takes the prisoner's tin mug and refills it with water from a bucket outside the door. Upon completing his task, he exits the cell and shuts the heavy door with a loud clang. Sergei consumes the welcome food. Afterwards, he sleeps fitfully until morning.

Sergei is awakened by the entrance of a guard into his cell. He is much refreshed from his period of sleep and intake of food, notwithstanding the aches he feels from lying on the hard wooden surface of the bench. The guard removes the previous day's tray and bowl. He places a fresh bowl of warm oatmeal gruel on the table. He refills the mug with fresh drinking water. Sergei assumes that it is morning. He has no way of knowing for sure. He no longer has a grip on the passage of time; the electric light burns continuously at a constant brightness; there is no natural daylight to serve as a reference. In the enclosed prison, his time is divided into periods of events, regardless of the actual time that elapses.

Sometime later, an hour perhaps, the guard escorts Sergei to the interrogation room. The setup is the same as before. The chief interrogator holds aloft Sergei's type-written report and his signed confession. He asks if he wishes to add anything to his report or make a qualifying statement. The prisoner replies by rendering a well-rehearsed statement of contrition and resolve. He expresses his desire to serve the common good through honourable labour.

The interrogator proclaims, "Comrade Sergei Murashko Falkov, for entertaining anti-Soviet principles, the Ministry of the Interior sentences you to eight years of honest labour in one or more corrective labour camps. Guard! Take the zek (prisoner) to his cell to await transportation."

Sergei's future looks bleak. He expects to labour with the literal hammer and sickle for the first time in his life.

CHAPTER FIVE

ONE POTATO, TWO POTATO, THREE POTATO, FOUR
(children's rhyme to determine 'it')

Lieutenant Denis Novak, chief administrator of Corrective Farm No.47, knocks his knuckles against his brow and stares down at his vacant desktop. "Where are the damn zeks?" he moans aloud. "The prison labourers should have arrived four weeks ago or, at worst, three." Farm No.47 is a forced-labour camp operating within the system of corrective labour camps. It is located in the Chuvashia Republic. The nearest settlement is the tiny hamlet of Bichurga-Baishevo, population circa 100, some 35 kilometres away. The lieutenant slaps his palm on the desk in frustration. "Don't those clowns in Moscow not realize that winter weather hits this region two weeks earlier than in the west."

Sergeant Vladimir Kotyakov, sitting opposite, coughs and smiles at the administrator's reference to 'clowns'. Normally, this expression of disrespect would be regarded as a punishable offence. But such sentiments are expressed, albeit with caution, when far removed from the critical eyes and ears of Moscow. The sergeant is sympathetic to the lieutenant's plight. If the potato crop is not harvested before the onset of winter, it will be lost. Sergeant Kotyakov is the farm administrator. He is a full-time resident of the farm. He has a staff of four under his supervision and is responsible for the management of the farm and its equipment.

Corrective Farm No.47 fulfills two purposes. The prison is responsible for the rehabilitation of inmates as prescribed by the Ministry of the Interior. The farm is required to produce food as per the quotas set by the Ministry of Agriculture. The prison and the farm are expected to function as a single coordinated operation. Today, this is clearly not the case.

Lieutenant Novak is not a full-time resident of the farm. He is assigned to administer the forced labour of the zek prisoners that are sent to toil here. A labour force is required at spring planting and harvest time. This is his first and current assignment to a farm labour camp. It is a test for him. If he performs well, he will be promoted; if he underperforms, he will be demoted.

The lieutenant rises from his chair and addresses the sergeant. "Tell me again, Comrade Sergeant, are we fully prepared?"

Vladimir is practical. He prefers to demonstrate with feet on the ground rather than submit written reports. "Come. Follow me. I will show you how prepared we are."

"That sounds like a 'no'."

"Comrade Lieutenant, we are fully prepared to gather the crop. But the harvest season is waning fast as winter approaches. Come. You must see for yourself."

"See what?"

They exit the solid brick building. The building serves as the prison. It also contains the administration offices and the sleeping quarters for the staff. Outside, an enormous yard is secured by a three-metre-high fence, isolating the compound from the surrounding land. The yard is square with a watchtower at each of the four corners. It is surfaced in a thin layer of stone chips. Wet mud oozes up between the stones and splatters their boots at each step. The surrounding farm buildings are wooden structures and are detached from the central brick building. They serve as storage barns for crops; they house farm machines and tools; one functions as a service garage and farm manager's office. A generator supplies the electrical requirements of the facility. A farm truck is parked next to the barns, and two delivery lorries are parked outside the garage.

Vladimir takes his superior officer on a tour of the farmyard. "See. The barns are cleaned out in preparation for the potato crop. And see over here, the transport lorries are tuned up and ready to ship the crops to the rail yards in Zelenodolsk. Even the farm truck is in an excellent state of repair. It's a pity it will not be used for this harvest."

"Why won't the truck be used if it is in excellent shape?"

"Why? Because the weather has turned wet and the fields have become muddy. Right now, the truck is unable to access the potato fields – the wheels will sink up to the axles before we go 50 metres."

"Ah. And the potato fields are five kilometres away."

"Yes. Five kilometres with no road access anywhere close. But not to worry. I have a contingency plan. Look inside the equipment shed." Vladimir slides open the door of the shed. Lieutenant Novak peers inside. The manager proudly exclaims, "Wicker creels! The potato crop will be carried on the backs of zeks all the way from the fields to the storage barn. With 150 zeks shouldering creels, we will move the potato crop just as quickly as with one truck – 150 creels equal one truckload."

"That is something I did not know. However, the zeks have not arrived yet. And I don't know how many are coming."

"They need to arrive soon. We are already halfway through October. I estimate that we have only two more weeks to dig the potatoes. The soil is already wet and heavy. Digging is onerous. Once the ground is saturated, we will not be able to continue the work. The fields get waterlogged in November. Then, when the frost arrives, the potatoes freeze in the ground…"

"…and the crop is destroyed."

"Exactly." The sergeant looks inquisitively at the lieutenant and asks, "As you see, I am ready, but are **you** ready, Comrade Lieutenant?" With that, Vladimir walks away from Denis Novak and into the service shed where he has his office.

Denis Novak makes no replay. He slowly walks past the little wooden huts where the farm manager and his staff live. They live, work and eat within the group of farm buildings like a community of monks. Denis, on the other hand, lives in the prison building in a private room. As he strides back to his office, he mentally checks his level of preparedness. Twenty prison guards are stationed in a state of readiness. In addition, he has 30 prison employees – cleaners, kitchen workers and maintenance staff. This latter group is a strange bunch.

Some are former prisoners; some others are soldiers working off their sentences for minor offences. In all, the labour camp population is comprised of guards, employees and soon-to-arrive zeks. Regardless of status, they are all workers, obliged to work 12-hour shifts. They sleep in identical dormitories; they eat the same food; they are confined within the prison complex (except when allocated to specific outdoor prison tasks). When off duty, they sometimes socialize together by drinking and singing and playing cards. It is possible to witness a guard and a zek, standing shoulder to shoulder, drinking together in song. However, some marked differences are maintained. The guards dress in standard army-issued uniforms. The prison workers wear the same uniforms except for the blue jackets worn in place of military tunics. The zeks dress in dark-blue work clothes and a mismatch of outdoor clothing when the temperature drops. Furthermore, the guards carry holstered handguns, which they discharge assuredly against anyone who breaks the rules. As for the others, the prison employees carry mops and buckets, the zeks carry shovels and spades. Lieutenant Novak continues to note his state of readiness. He has sufficient work uniforms for the incoming zeks. And sufficient food, if one regards potatoes and cabbage as sufficient food. Once a week, a slice of dried fish is added to the diet. Yes, he is fully prepared – except for the crew of zek workers he urgently needs.

Back in his office, Denis Novak notices the envelope on his desk. This means that the driver has returned from Zelenyj Dol Station with the post. He hastily opens the envelope. "A-hah!" he exclaims aloud. The letter informs him that the allotted zek labourers will arrive tomorrow, transported in army lorries. "At last!" he says and sits down in relief.

*   *   *   *   *

Meanwhile, in Moscow's Kazansky Railway Station, 1,070 kilometres away and 24 hours by rail and lorry, Sergei Falkov is boarding a railcar. He is among a group of prisoners bound for forced-labour camps. He is unable to estimate the number of prisoners, but certainly more than 100. Three railcars are engaged to accommodate the motley collection. The guards prod the zeks with poles to crowd them into the cars. The interior of Sergei's car has shelves. To maximize the numbers that can be boarded, prisoners are required to lie on the shelves tiered three deep. Zeks, like Sergei, who are deemed to hold anti-Soviet sentiments, are ordered to stand on the floor. The last zek to be pushed into the car is a burly man with his hands tied behind his back. The guards brutally beat him as he struggles to resist.

He shouts at them defiantly, "I am a hero of the Revolution! Comrade Lenin personally presented me with a medal. Let me go!"

The guards beat him all the more. He stumbles face down onto the floor of the car. A guard pulls the slipknot of his bonds to release his arms. Thereupon, the guard jumps from the car and his companions slide the door shut before the brute has time to recover. The train starts to move. The brute is dazed. He rolls over with the motion of the train. He manages to stand erect. His face is bloodied. He raves at the occupants of the car. "What are you looking at?" and punches the closest prisoner in the face. The prisoner's nose splatters blood and the surprised zek falls to the floor. The brute commences swinging punches at all those within reach. However, he is unable to maintain his balance as the train picks up speed. Four prisoners pounce on him, pinning his arms and legs. They wrestle him to the floor with the help of the swaying car. A fifth prisoner strangles the brute with his bare hands. The massive man bucks violently but he is unable to shake himself free. In a short time, he goes limp. The five assailants continue to hold him down for over a minute to ensure that he is truly dead. The occupants of the car stare at the fallen giant with bated breath. They are fearful that he might revive and go berserk. Minutes pass. A zek, who was previously a medical doctor, confirms that the man is dead. He then attends to the fallen zek with the bleeding nose and helps him to his feet. As things calm down, the prisoners settle in for their journey to unknown destinations.

Fifteen hours later, the train stops. The door of the car opens. A guard loudly calls the names of those required to disembark. "Sergei Falkov! Out!" And so on. When the list is completed, two guards enter the car to inspect it. They discover the dead body. They do not appear to be disturbed by the death of a prisoner. They remove the dead man by dragging him and rolling him out through the open doorway. As the guards depart, one prisoner bravely shouts after them, "What about me? Am I on the list? My name is Anton…"

The guards shut the door. One guard shouts for the benefit of Anton, the man who asked the question. "Next stop, Vladivostok!"

Sergei and the other selected zeks are assembled into three rows, four deep. Thereupon, they are marched to three waiting army lorries where they are boarded like cattle. The last to enter each lorry are two soldiers with rifles. Sergei is in the third lorry. He notices that the zek doctor and the man with the bloody nose are on board with him. The soldiers lift the tailgate and secure it in place, then slap it loudly for the driver to hear the signal to move off. Sergei looks around to establish his whereabouts. As they depart from the railway siding, he perceives that he is in Zelenodolsk, some 50 kilometres east of the city of Kazan. Throughout the nine-hour journey, he looks for road signs that might give him a clue of the route. They pass Shemursha in the Chuvashia Republic. Later, he glimpses a sign pointing east to the town of Malobuyanovskoye. Sergei knows that this is in the region of Shemurshinskiy Rayon, deeper in the Chuvashia Republic. An hour later they reach their destination. The lorry drives past a metal gate and into a muddy yard. Plainly, it is a huge farmyard with a collection of wooden buildings, except for the imposing brick building in the centre. The compound is encircled by a high barbed-wire fence. Sergei deduces that it is a labour camp on a farm, not unusual since the establishment of collective farming. But it could be worse. He is thankful that he did not continue on the train to Vladivostok. The unfortunate zeks that are sent to the Siberian east coast seldom return. Here, on this farm in the Chuvashia Republic, his chances of surviving are much better.

CHAPTER SIX

FIVE POTATO, SIX POTATO, SEVEN POTATO, MORE

Lieutenant Denis Novak goes to the yard to greet the incoming army lorries. The vehicles park, side by side, at the entrance to the prison building. The sergeant in charge of the convoy strides up to him and salutes. "Comrade Lieutenant, a delivery of zeks for you." With that, he turns his attention to the lorries. "Everybody out!" he shouts. "Line up here in front as your name is called." He consults a clipboard and calls out each zek's name. When he is finished, he proclaims, "All present and correct!" He removes the top sheet from the clipboard and gives it to Lieutenant Novak together with an attached brown envelope. He has him sign a copy of the delivery confirmation. Thereupon, he salutes once more and turns on his heel. He waves at the lorries to depart.

"Wait!" This is the first word Denis Novak utters since the arrival of the lorries. "Sergeant, you have delivered 80 zeks. This is half the expected number. When will the others arrive?"

"The others? I deliver what I was ordered to deliver. It is stated in the delivery document."

"Yes, of course. Let me examine it closely. Meanwhile, you and your men may rest for a while and avail of some food before your return journey."

The army sergeant and his nine soldiers are escorted into the building. Lieutenant Novak and a contingent of eight guards view the line of zeks. The prisoners stand in single file. He consults the list. Where he had expected 150 able-bodied workers, he is presented with 80 weaklings. None of these zeks appear capable of physical work. According to the list, they range in age from 48 to 59. They are dishevelled and sickly. He addresses the newcomers. "This is a corrective labour facility. And it is a farm. Whenever you assemble or stand in line, or queue up, you do so in this order." This ensures that the prisoners are lined in alphabetical order as per the list. "Now follow the guards' instructions."

The prisoner-to-guard to ratio is ten to one. The zeks are herded into eight units of ten. They are ordered to strip. Their dirty clothing is thrown in a heap for burning. A small number of garments are deemed acceptable and are put aside. Sergei stands shivering in the open farmyard. Cold mud oozes up from the ground and seeps between his bare toes. He looks at the guard who rummages through his discarded clothes. The guard checks the prisoner's wallet of Moroccan leather. It is empty except for the rail pass and a photograph of Anne Brennan. He chucks the items on the pile to be burned, followed by the English shoes and the remainder of Sergei's clothing. He removes the prisoner's glasses and examines them. He is curious about the strangely-shaped eyepieces. Instead of being circular, the lenses are semicircular and are suspended from horizontal frames that look like thick brown eyebrows. He returns the glasses to Sergei – the only item to survive the inspection. After this ordeal, the prisoners are marched inside the building for delousing. In the bathroom, they are ordered to lather their entire bodies in lye soap and rinse off by dipping fully into baths of cold water. Prisoners have their heads shaved. Sergei, who is balding and has a thin line of short hair, is excluded from this treatment. His goatee and facial hair are not regarded as a louse problem. After the delousing treatment, the prisoners are brought to piles of clothing – used items from former inmates. Sergei notices that the clothing is clean and dry – a welcome surprise. He selects long underwear and shirts, a long tunic of dark blue, matching trousers, a quilted jacket, boots of the correct size, mittens and a hat with flaps. When he has assembled his selection of clothes, he is escorted, still naked, to a dormitory. The rows of iron-framed beds are arranged in the same order as the names on the list. Each bed is padded with a horse-hair mattress and is dressed in clean sheets and a single grey wool blanket. A wooden storage trunk is located at the foot of each bed. The zeks are ordered to dress in their dark-blue labour uniforms and place their remaining clothing in their respective storage boxes. Sergei glances at his neighbour zek and nods towards the bed. The zek smiles back. They both look at the beds and trunks and acknowledge that this is a degree of comfort unexpected in a prison. In truth, it is superior to what most peasants enjoy. Once dressed, the zeks are ordered to the communal dining room. Here, they queue for broth – a full ladle of hot thick potato soup – and bread. After eating, the zeks are escorted back to the dormitory to retire for the night.

At first, the zeks lie quietly for fear of attracting the attention of the guards. After a while, they begin to whisper to each other and speak softly. Surprisingly, no guard comes to punish those who dare to speak. One brave zek steals out of his bed and checks the dormitory door. He is amazed to discover that it is unlocked. Another zek, eager to outperform his comrade's bravery, opens the door and peers out. He is immediately addressed by a guard on duty in the hallway. The guard assumes that the zek wishes to avail of a toilet, and directs him to the appropriate room at the end of the corridor. Upon learning this, some of the zeks plot to escape. If the guards are this lax, it should be easy.

In the administration office, Lieutenant Denis Novak

sits at his desk and reads the contents of the brown envelope. It contains new orders about the crop harvest. The import of the newly-acquired orders weighs heavily on him. He is distressed. To fulfill his orders, he needs an adequate supply of manpower. Alas, the number of newly-arrived zeks is too few. And they are insufficiently fit to perform the required work. He reads through the list of zeks for the umpteenth time – former accountants, clerks, teachers and other soft professionals. He whispers through clenched teeth, "Damn those Moscow clowns." To make matters worse, his new orders set his quota at six railcars of potatoes. Six empty railcars are already in position on a siding at Zelenyj Dol Station to receive the goods. And, worse still, 01 November is the delivery deadline – 17 days hence. He asks himself, "Do these Moscow clowns think that the required crop of potatoes is lying in storage, awaiting loading and transportation to the rail siding?" The entire crop is still in the ground, five kilometres away. He sighs heavily in the face of an overwhelming task. He removes his sidearm from its holster and spins it recklessly on the desktop. The gun comes to rest with the barrel pointing ominously at the dejected administrator.

The next morning, the zeks are awakened before dawn. For breakfast, they are served bread and a half-ladle of cabbage soup. They don their outdoor clothing and line up in the farmyard for their first day of manual labour. Each zek is provided with a spade and a wicker creel. They are marched, ten by ten, three abreast, to the potato fields five kilometres away. Drizzle blows against their faces as they trudge with heavy feet. The weather is usual for the time of year. The rain moistens the ground underfoot and renders it muddy and slick. The zeks slip and slide and frequently lose their footing in the unfamiliar terrain. Eventually, they learn to walk confidently and fall into step with the guards.

Sergei is in group number three, marching alongside group number six. The ground is rendered slicker by the tramping of the groups farther ahead. He looks to see if his group is keeping up with those in front. Suddenly, three zeks break away from group number two and make for a wooded area. Three rapid shots break the silence and the three escaping zeks drop dead. They had managed to run a mere two paces on the slippery ground.

"Everybody down!" the guards shout. "Down, down! Facedown!" Sergei throws himself flat in the mud and remains motionless. After a few seconds of silence, the guards shout some more. "Everyone up! Resume walking!" Sergei and the zeks are now smeared with mud from head to toe. But this incident has shocked them back into reality. They are prisoners. And prisoners are shot when they step out of line. The guards decide to leave the three dead zeks where they fell 'as a sign to others'. As Sergei walks past the dead men, he is impressed by the accuracy of the shots. Each dead zek has a single bullet wound in the upper torso. Three rapid shots; three dead zeks.

The remaining work crew of 77, plus their 8 escorts, continue onward to the distant potato fields. Sergei learns how to use his spade to balance his footing and masters a steady gait. He views the surrounding landscape. He is puzzled by the huge tract of empty land they traverse through. Why are the potatoes planted so far from the farm? Why not plant them in the field close by? The answer, he presumes, must lie in the inefficiencies of ministerial commissioners that impose untested policies from a distance. Who, in Moscow, would know the best location in the region of Shemurshinskiy Rayon in which to plant potatoes?

After walking for an hour and a half, the zeks reach the potato fields. This has taken longer than planned. Had there been favourable ground conditions, they would have walked the distance within an hour. Consequently, the work is delayed.

Sergei casts his eyes over the vast area of cultivated

land. The potatoes are planted in rows of narrow drills. The withered potato stalks protrude from the ground, thus marking the location of the tubers below. Each zek is directed to a drill and ordered to dig. Sergei follows the instructions. He digs into the soil. He is surprised by the weight of the dirt. It is wet. And it clings to the blade of the spade. It is an effort to loosen the soil and heave it. When the soil breaks apart, the exposed potatoes tumble out. Next, he gathers the potatoes in his hands and tosses them into his creel. He repeats this task two more times to fill the creel. Then, as directed, he jams his spade upright in the ground to mark his spot. He shoulders his filled creel and joins the other members of his group. Thereupon, they proceed back to the farm. Sergei finds the going tough. This time, he has no spade to use as a walking stick. The weight of the creel throws him off balance. He slips and falls. The contents of the creel spill out. To punish him for his clumsiness, the guard strikes him with a stick. He hurriedly refills his creel and resumes walking. The other zeks experience the same difficulty. Each time a zek falls over and loses his load, he is beaten. The accompanying zeks assist in retrieving the spilled potatoes. Progress is slow. When the farm comes into view, Sergei is encouraged to reach his goal without further punishment. In his exuberance, he slips and falls backwards. Not only does he lose his load, but he also breaks the side of the wicker creel. The guard hits him and orders him to use his inner tunic to line the torn basket. Sergei carries and drags the creel the last few metres to the farmyard. The walk back to the farm has taken them more than two painful hours. The zeks unload their creels in the storage shed and prepare to return to the potato fields to repeat the entire process. The guard orders Sergei to choose a fresh creel from the stack in the barn. When he reaches the stacked creels, the fatigued zek leans on them to rest his body. The impatient guard approaches him threateningly.

Sergei turns to face the guard and says, "This is a disaster. It is inefficient and senseless."

The guard strikes him and asks sarcastically, "So, you have a better way? Eh?"

Between blows, Sergei declares, "Yes! Ten times more efficient…"

"Enough!"

For his insolence, Sergei is placed in a cooling-off cell to spend a day without food or water.

*   *   *   *   *

That evening, Denis Novak, the lieutenant

administrator, requests the daily progress report. He summons the farm manager and the head guard of the work detail to his office. He addresses Vladimir Kotyakov. "Comrade Sergeant, how much crop did we manage to gather today?"

"Not much, Comrade Lieutenant. The zeks succeeded in making two round trips within a ten-hour shift. The number of potatoes collected and stored today amounts to no more than a single truckload."

"What?" Denis rises from his chair in anger. "One whole day for 80 zeks to collect just one truckload of potatoes?"

"Not 80 zeks – just 77. And tomorrow, just 76."

"So, I cannot expect an improvement tomorrow?"

"I'm afraid not."

Lieutenant Denis Novak needs every zek to work in the fields. He asks, "Explain '76'?"

"Three were shot dead."

Denis turns to the guard. "Is this so?"

The guard swallows. "Yes, Comrade Lieutenant. Three zeks were shot and killed when they attempted to escape.”

Denis nods. This is the correct punishment. He approves. “And the other?”

The guard is emboldened by the administrator's reaction; it is obvious that he supports the enforcement of just punishment. “He was insolent. A day without food or water will discipline him.”

Lieutenant Novak resumes his seat. He is suddenly weary. He asks the guard to elaborate. “A zek was insolent? And what did he say that warrants a day in a cell – an entire day off work?”

“He said that we are stupid and that he could find a way to increase our efficiency tenfold.” The guard laughs derisively. “Imagine. A zek telling us how to operate a labour camp.”

The administrator accepts the guard's reasoning. He turns his attention back to Vladimir. “The figures. Give me the figures. Where are we at, and what is our progress?”

“Based on today's performance, we collected a truckload of potatoes. Now, one lorry equals four tucks. And it takes six lorries to fill one railcar. As I figure, it would take 24 days to fill one railcar. Even if we can double our output, which I doubt, it would take…"

"…12 days to fill one railcar. With just 16 days to our deadline, we can expect to load between two-thirds and one-and-a-third railcars." Denis suspects that the ministry sets the quotas deliberately high to encourage farms to strive harder. If the bar is set low, there is the risk of underperformance. His quota is set at six railcars, probably in expectation of five. By providing five cars of potatoes, he has a good chance of keeping his position. Six would garner him a promotion. Three or four would probably result in his demotion. Under 50% and he might be sentenced to a labour camp as a zek. And now he is looking at realizing just one meagre railcar of potatoes. A failure at this extreme would surely result in the ultimate punishment. If he is to be shot, he hopes that it will be in the head. They say it's painless. He takes his sidearm, as he did on the previous evening, and spins it on the desk. The other two men fall to the floor, out of harm's way, should the gun discharge. When the spinning gun comes to a stop, Vladimir rises and peers at it. He gingerly moves the barrel to point away from any potential human target. The two men resume their seats in silence and look at the lieutenant for an explanation. Denis fingers the gun, rocking it gently to and fro, while deep in thought. Suddenly, he replaces his sidearm in its holster and speaks. "The prisoner, the zek in the cell, which one is he?"

The guard musters enough confidence to reply. "Which one is he? His name is Sergei Falkov."

The administrator consults the list of zeks. He scans down to the letter F and places his finger on the name 'Sergei Falkov'. He reads the accompanying one-line description and notes the prisoner's former occupation – 'inventor'. He raises his eyes and looks squarely at the guard. "And you say that this zek, Sergei Falkov, stated that he could increase our efficiency ten-fold?"

The guard laughs nervously. He is disturbed by the administrator's strange behaviour. "Yes. But that's insane. He was just mouthing off…"

Denis cuts him off. "Bring him here!"

"Comrade Lieutenant?"

"Bring the prisoner Sergei Falkov here, this minute!"

The startled guard jumps to his feet. "Yes, Comrade Lieutenant." And he hastily departs from the room.

Moments later, the guard re-enters escorting a much-bruised zek. Lieutenant Novak dismisses the guard and directs his attention to the prisoner. "You are Prisoner Sergei Falkov?"

To Sergei, this is just one more stage in the process of his punishment. He expects to be questioned on his 'anti-Soviet views' and lectured on rehabilitation. He renders a reflex response. "Yes, Comrade."

"Sit."

Sergei sits in the chair recently vacated by the guard. He senses an unusual atmosphere. He recognizes the man who addresses him. It is the prison administrator. He saw him in the yard when they first arrived at the prison. An army sergeant is seated next to Sergei. If the sergeant is seated next to him and not at the far side of the desk, Sergei construes that it cannot be an interrogation. He steals a sideways glance at the sergeant's face. He recognizes him as a member of the farm staff. If this is not a standard questioning, he wonders what is going on. The administrator studies Sergei for a moment. Perhaps he is moved by the puffed bruises visible on the zek's face. Sergei is surprised when he poses an unexpected question. "Comrade Falkov, would you like a drink of water?"

"Yes, Comrade…"

"…Lieutenant. I am Lieutenant Denis Novak. I am in charge here."

"Yes, Comrade Lieutenant. I would like some water to drink."

Denis maintains his eyes on the prisoner. Studying him; sizing him up. He shouts, loud enough to be heard in the adjoining office. "Guard! Bring water for the prisoner!"

A junior guard enters with a mug of drinking water. He offers it to the zek. Sergei gratefully consumes the water. The guard exits and shuts the door. Denis leans forward over the desk and asks, "Increase our efficiency ten-fold? That's what you said, is it not? Explain."

Sergei is refreshed by the water. He is now fully cognizant of the nature of the meeting. It isn't an interrogation; it is a work-strategy meeting. And he is invited to contribute. "Comrade Lieutenant, I believe that the current method of gathering the potato crop is inefficient. And I have suggestions, which if you entertain, would greatly improve the process."

"By ten-fold?"

"Eventually. But not at first. I would recommend implementing a five-step improvement plan." Sergei is animated by the opportunity to express his ideas. "The first step is two-pronged. It could be put in place within a day."

The sergeant turns to him and asks, "And what is this two-pronged first step?"

"Division of labour. Organize the zeks into work units of five. Place five creels in a row on the ground alongside the drill. Man number one digs, not lifts, using the spade as a lever to push out the soil. The potatoes will break from the soil and spill. Man number two gathers the potatoes and throws them into the creels. And so on, working along the drill. Meanwhile, the other three men carry the filled creels, empty them, and return the now-empty creels to be next in line and ready to be filled. For relief, rotate the workers within the unit. Do this. It is faster and uses less equipment – one spade per five zeks."

Lieutenant Novak and Vladimir nod in agreement. Vladimir poses a question. "I see how this speeds up the process of harvesting the crop, but how does it help in transporting the potatoes to the storage barns? We are still unable to carry the crop from the fields to the farm any faster. This is the major problem that we must overcome."

Sergei lifts his finger and says, "I am not finished. I said that it is two-pronged. Secondly, the zeks carry the potatoes from the drill to the truck nearby."

Vladimir turns and guffaws at Sergei. "Hah! Carry the potatoes to the truck nearby? The farm truck cannot travel on the muddy ground to the fields. There **is** no truck nearby!"

Sergei responds with equal enthusiasm. "Oh yes, there is! On the boards."

Vladimir tries to speak but is unable to find the words. Denis jumps in with a question. "What do you mean 'On the boards'?"

"The truck cannot travel on the mud. We know that. But it can travel on boards placed on the mud."

This time, Vladimir finds words. "You mean to place boards on the mud for the truck to travel from the farm to the fields? What? For five kilometres?"

"No. Six boards of the correct length and thickness and width. Six zeks would run with the truck placing the boards under the wheels as it progresses. As the truck clears a pair of boards, the men would carry them to the front of the moving truck. And so on. The men would tire quickly, so relay teams would be needed. Probably three teams in total, holding onto the truck and riding the running boards while resting."

Sergei falls silent. The two men look at each other. They struggle to comprehend the concept. A discussion ensues between the administrator and the farm manager. Sergei manages to insert a comment. "It is the same principle as a pontoon bridge." The two men look at him for a moment. After a brief pause, they resume their discussion. In the end, they conclude that Sergei's proposal is fraught with difficulties and is unlikely to succeed. However, Lieutenant Denis Novak decides that there is nothing to lose by trying it. Even if it fails, he is no worse off. And there is the remote chance of success, however unlikely. He orders Sergei to work under the supervision of the farm manager and put his pontoon-board plan to a practical test.

CHAPTER SEVEN

POTATOES ONBOARD

Next morning, Sergei is brought to the service garage where the farm manager's office is located and where he will work on his project. Vladimir introduces him to the farm staff. There are four in addition to the manager himself. He meets Pyotr, Gregori, Boris and Mikhail. Everyone is on first-name terms. Notwithstanding his zek status, they treat him as a fellow worker. Sergei isn't sure if titles are dispensed with, in the spirit of the Revolution, or if the men are lax. Lenin insisted on dropping all references to rank, favouring a form of address that recognizes a person's position. For example, 'Officer' became 'Administrator'. Under Stalin, some references to rank are permitted to avoid confusion. 'Lieutenant-Administrator' is permitted, as is 'Sergeant-Manager'. Vladimir might address Boris as 'Mechanic' at one time and as 'Carpenter' later on. And seeing that they all share the work, any one of the men could be 'Mechanic' or 'Carpenter' as required. It is much easier to address them by given name.

Sergei likes the garage. It contains a miscellaneous collection of machine parts for repairing farm equipment. It has a fully-stocked carpenter's shop with shelves stacked high with lumber. The garage is huge enough to fit two lorries with room to spare. There are three backrooms, side by side – two storage rooms and the manager's office. A stove is located next to the office. The men cook their food here. There is always a pot of 'tea' on the hotplate. The men call it 'tea', but it is a very thin soup made from potato skins. Still, it is a refreshing hot drink to be consumed at will. Each man has his personal mug, plate and utensils. They present Sergei with his own utensils. The white enamelled mug is bent at the side but serves its purpose. At mealtimes, they eat potatoes, cabbage and dried fish. They cook the dried fish in the cabbage water. Instead of tables and chairs, they use whatever is at hand – a workbench, lorry tires, wooden boxes or just a heap of wooden planks.

The men are curious about Sergei's purpose. Vladimir enlightens them. They are interested in Sergei's plan and are keen to help.

Sergei asks Vladimir about the location of the potato fields and why they are located so far away, seeing that there are fields much closer.

Vladimir replies, "Far? No, they are not far, only five kilometres. They are easily accessed at the proper harvest time. That is in early September when digging is easy, back when the truck can make many trips in a single day. You know, the entire harvest can be stored in three weeks. But after the first week of October… Hah."

"But why not plant the potatoes closer to the farmyard where the storage barns are located?"

"We do, sometimes. You see, it's all to do with crop rotation. Root crops one year, grain the next and grazing in the third year. What you walked past yesterday were the oat fields. But the oats were harvested in August. That was by a different bunch of zeks."

"Oats? I thought that this was just a potato farm."

"Ah, no. This is all part of the corrective farm system. The zeks come here only when we need the labour. They come for a while. And then they are off to someplace else. It is a mobile workforce. But let me tell you, when you said that this might be just a potato farm, you were almost right. You see, the grazing is for the benefit of the Bichurga-Baishevo Collective Farm – part of the cooperation between farms. The oats are for domestic consumption. But the potatoes are for export."

The potatoes are for export. Sergei sees the poetic justice and wonders if being sent here has a particular point. Back in Moscow, Dmitry Reshetnikov referred to potatoes in his parting remark.

Vladimir changes the subject and draws attention to the task at hand. "Sergei, tell us your plan. Do you want to build pontoon boards for the truck so that it can travel on mud? Well, if you have the plans, we have the lumber."

"Ah, yes. First I need to draw up the plans on paper so that I can show you the diagram."

"You want paper? In my office."

"And pencils, ruler, protractor, compass, set squares."

"All from the carpenter's tools. Make yourself at home in my office. It has a desk and a real chair."

A short time later, Sergei hands a drawing to Vladimir. The others flock around to examine it. They understand it and set to work. In less than half an hour, the first sample model is complete. They test it for strength and suitability. It fails the strength test. The weight of a fully laden truck would bend it. Sergei makes modifications. Other models are constructed of varying thicknesses and lengths and widths. Finally, a board is constructed which is light enough to be carried, yet reinforced with ribs to maintain a rigid strength. It passes the strength test. But the surface is smooth and the truck tires skid off the board when slick with mud. Ridges, like rungs of a ladder, are fixed to the surface of the board. This solves the problem. The board passes the truck test, but the weight of the truck imbeds the board into the soft ground. It is a time-consuming effort to free the board and relocate it. So, the board is fitted with handles and ropes. Thereafter, it is easily dislodged from the muddy ground and lifted or dragged to a new position. Satisfied with the sample, they quickly construct a set of six boards.

Next, they take the truck out to the fields for an onsite test. They enlist the guards and prison employees to ride in the bed of the truck to match a full load. Six more guards act as zek runners. There is a sense of excitement as in a sporting challenge. The truck succeeds in travelling a kilometre in a wide circle over muddy ground. It returns to the farmyard to the cheers of the participating guards. The shouts arrest the attention of the administrator. Denis Novak comes out of the building to investigate. Rather than explain the success of the trial, Vladimir urges the administrator to ride in the truck to experience the success firsthand. Denis is infected with the same excitement as the men. He raises his arms and the guards haul him up and into the bed of the truck. Guards vie with each other for the honour of acting as 'runner zeks' and the truck executes another successful circuitous kilometre. When they arrive back in the farmyard, the administrator issues instructions to modify the work routine to accommodate the changes – divide the zeks into work units of five and utilize the truck to transport the potato crop from the fields. Thus, step one of Sergei's plan is put into action.

Sergei is not present at the celebration. He is already back in Vladimir's office. He is enthused with the first step of his plan and is vigorously working on the succeeding steps. He is already settled in and regards the manager's office as his personal workspace. He becomes familiar with the contents – typewriter, drawing paper, paper with letterhead, blank forms of waybills. In a short time, the office is strewn with his drawings and charts. He pins sheets of paper to the corkboard and sticks them on the wall beside a row of hooks. Keys dangle from the hooks, identified by labels. At a quick glance, Sergei recognizes keys for the lorries and keys for the storage barns and ancillary buildings. And why not, he thinks. After all, this is the farm manager's office. But nothing in the manager's office pertains to the prison.

On the following day, the new work routine is a success. Sergei is present with the farm manager at the daily meeting in the administrator's office. Denis is pleased with the report – three truckloads of potatoes delivered to the storage barn. At this rate, he will succeed in filling two railcars by the deadline. It's not enough, but it is a step in the right direction. He poses a question to Sergei. "Comrade Falkov…" Sergei notes that 'Prisoner' is omitted from the form of address. "…you have a second step to your plan?"

"Yes, Comrade Administrator. Here is a set of drawings." Sergei hands a set of drawings to both men. "In step two we will fix removable side panels to the farm truck. This will increase the load by 250%…"

Denis raises his eyes in surprise and interrupts. "Do you mean two-and-a-half times a normal truckload? Is this possible? And how did you come up with this idea?"

Sergei renders an unexpected reply. "Not my idea at all. I was calculating the top speed of the farm truck when loaded. It cannot travel faster than the time it takes for the runner-zeks to reposition the boards – roughly at walking speed. To increase productivity, we need to increase the capacity of the truck. Vladimir had the solution"

Denis turns to the farm manager and asks, "So this is your idea?"

Vladimir speaks plainly. "It's not an idea. This is what we do to transport a light load. We used the extended side panels in August to transport the oats. So, not just possible; it is tried and true. The panels are already installed and will be used on tomorrow's loads."

The administrator is digesting this information. He scribbles on his copy of the plan. "You say 'to transport a light load'. Are potatoes a light load? At 250% normal load capacity?"

Vladimir continues to speak factually. "A load of potatoes is semi-heavy – too heavy at 250% for normal speed. To transport a load as proposed by Sergei, the truck would need to operate in first gear for the entire journey. And first gear is…"

"…is at walking speed." Lieutenant Denis Novak grasps the practicality of the plan.

Sergei is impatient to resume his presentation. He picks up where he left off. "As I was saying, each truckload will henceforth by equal to 250% of a normal load. But there is more to this. Currently, the pontoon-boards permit the truck to move forward or, if required, reverse – but only in a straight line. Tight turns are impossible. To turn around, the truck needs to travel in a wide circle. If you study page two, you see a plan for a horizontal platform of stout planks. This will be installed at the potato field where the truck is loaded. With this platform, the truck can execute a three-point turn, a full 180°, for the return trip."

Once more, Vladimir interjects. "The planks are already loaded on the truck. We will bring them to the fields for the first load."

Sergei is annoyed at the interruptions. He resumes speaking. "As you can see from the specifications, the planks are easily positioned and are easily relocated. The turning point for the truck will always be in the vicinity of the digging – for quick loading. So, the turn-around time for each truck journey is reduced. This will increase the number of completed trips. I estimate a 333% increase in productivity after tomorrow."

Denis Novak is visibly excited. "Let me get this. Are you saying that, as of tomorrow, productivity will be 333% of the first day?"

"No. Tomorrow will realize 250% of today's yield; the following day will attain 333% of today's yield – or 1,000% of day one. This brings me to step three. I refer you to the next page. Bear in mind that, after tomorrow, the delivery of potatoes from the fields to the farm will exceed the daily capacity of the two transport lorries.

Because of the distance from the farm to the rail siding, each lorry can make just one round trip per day. Here is a detailed sketch of a proposed trailer to be fitted to the rear of each transport lorry. The parts required to assemble the trailers are available from the service garage – wheels, lumber and so on. Upon completion, the transportation capacity of each lorry will increase by 50%. Whereas it currently takes six lorryloads to fill a single railcar, henceforth it will take just four."

Denis grasps the significance of the information. He exclaims, "A railcar filled every two days?" He writes additional notes.

Sergei cautions him. "Not quite. We still need to increase the rate at which the crop is moved from the fields to the farmyard. That is step four, which will be set up tomorrow and be fully functional on the following day.

"But I am getting ahead of myself. Let's get back to step three. Currently, we store the potatoes in a barn until we accumulate a lorryload. This is inefficient. The potatoes should be transferred directly from the farm truck to the transport lorries. Store only the overload portion in the barn.

"When the modifications of step three are executed, I

will present step four. And, after that, step five. If you carry out all five steps, I predict that we will fill five railcars by the deadline."

"Five railcars filled by the deadline? Is that really possible?" Denis isn't sure if he should believe it or not.

Sergei continues with his presentation. "As I say, there is more to be done. At this point, I need to get a full understanding of the weather and how it affects conditions in the fields. To do this, I need to work closely with Vladimir. Together, we make a resourceful team. My main issue, as yet unresolved, is with non-productive time in the fields while awaiting the arrival of the truck. The downtime should be put to good use. I will give you my recommendations tomorrow evening."

The administrator is startled by the reference to 'downtime'. "What do you mean by 'downtime'? Surely, the zeks are not idle at any time."

Vladimir jumps in quickly to clarify. "Comrade Administrator, there is never any idle time during the work period. There is a 20-minute break at the midpoint when the zeks are given cold cabbage soup. The 'downtime' that Sergei refers to is the period from when the truck departs from the field to when it returns. During that period, the truck cannot be filled."

"So how are the zeks employed during these periods?"

"Today, the guards had them walk in circles carrying fully-laden creels."

"That's good. It is important for the rehabilitation of the zeks that they experience manual labour to the point of exhaustion."

Sergei exclaims with obvious irritation, "The downtime is unproductive. Regardless, this will be rectified tomorrow."

Vladimir adds, "And if we experience any further downtime, the zeks will be put to digging pits."

This explanation appears to appease the administrator. He responds to Sergei. "You will present step four and step five tomorrow?" Denis notes the absence of 'Comrade' when Sergei refers to Vladimir. He writes 'disrespect' on the sheet of paper. He reconsiders. He scribbles; obliterates the word and writes 'camaraderie?'

"Yes. I will have the final steps tomorrow." Sergei regards this as the conclusion of his presentation.

Denis is anxious to see how the following day progresses. And if it will produce the projected results.

CHAPTER EIGHT

FIVE STEPS

On the following day, Sergei and Vladimir are working side by side. Step three is underway. The turning platform is built in the fields next to the digging area. The truck, now at 250% load capacity, manages to complete a round trip in a little over three hours. During the course of the day, Gregori executes three successful trips. This equates to seven-and-a-half regular truckloads. Meanwhile, Pyotr, Boris and Mikhail are tasked with building trailers for the two lorries. This is a simple task for men who are experienced in repairing motor-vehicle equipment and in carpentry. They obtain the necessary spare wheels and suitable lumber in the service garage. An old wrecked farm truck is quickly converted into a trailer.

Sergei and Vladimir are far away, albeit physically close. They are deep into planning the next two steps. Sergei makes proposals, some of which are unfeasible. Vladimir recommends practical modifications. Drawings pass back and forth until a viable design is agreed upon. Finally, they decide on a device that will load the farm truck rapidly – an elevated box with an openable panel. Ten boxes will be erected in the fields at the truck's turning point. The boxes need to be high enough to tip their contents into the bed of the truck and have a step-up for the zeks to empty their baskets into them. The clever feature is in the angle of the base of each box. The floor is sloped at 7° and the moveable front panel functions as a drawbridge when opened into position. Notwithstanding, it is a simple construction – a wooden box on stilt-like legs sitting at an angle of 7°. Vladimir estimates that the boxes will be built and installed by the end of the day. When operational, the truck will simply pull up alongside the loaded boxes and the potatoes will be released into the truck bed. The estimated time to fill the farm truck is one minute. As a result of the time saved, the number of daily loads will increase from three to four. Compared to what was transported solely in baskets on the first day, this is ten times greater.

It is mid-day. Sergei and Vladimir take a break to consume hot watery potato soup. During the break, Vladimir questions Sergei on his past and asks him how he got sentenced to forced labour. Vladimir is not surprised that time spent in America would result in such an ignominious outcome. Sergei, in turn, questions Vladimir on his work as a farm manager. Vladimir describes the purpose of the farm and how it relies on intermittent forced labour throughout the year. Despite the relationship between the prison and the farm, there is a disconnection. Vladimir describes it. "The current prison administrator has a limited understanding of the farm operation. He focuses on the rehabilitation of zeks, and 'rehabilitation' often means 'working to death'. His overriding goal is to reach an unattainable quota. Failure could have disastrous consequences for him. Consequently, zeks are subjected to brutal treatment to maximize productivity. Many die from the gruelling work. But a zek's life has little value and zeks are easily replaced. Very few zeks live to see the completion of an eight-year sentence." Vladimir pauses to consume his potato tea. He looks at Sergei's slight build and says, "I can't see you surviving a year of forced labour."

Sergei is brought down to earth with a thud. For as long as he provides ideas to increase productivity, he is safe. But in the end, he is just a zek – considered to be an anti-Soviet dissident. And someday he will likely be thrust back into forced physical labour. He resolves to come up with a plan to survive.

Vladimir breaks his reverie with a comment. "Come, I have an idea. It should dovetail into your step five."

"An idea?

"Have you considered potato pits?"

Sergei and Vladimir catch a ride on the truck. They

share the ride with Boris and Gregori. The first five boxes are onboard ready for rapid assembly at the fields. The remaining five will be delivered later in the day with the final trip of the truck. Boris is talkative. He relates how, in the early morning, they were able to construct one trailer. A second trailer is under construction. One trailer is ready to be hitched to a lorry for the next delivery to the rail siding. And now the boxes are also ready.

Upon reaching the fields, the zeks are employed in erecting the boxes. Boris and Gregori oversee the work to ensure that the supporting legs are firmly secured and that the sloping angle of each box is at least 7°. The workers might attempt to level the boxes to sit horizontally.

Vladimir says to Sergei, "Come. You told me that you wanted to talk about the weather." They walk through the muddy fields to the furthermost side. "Sergei, I was looking at your ideas for the final stage of your big plan. You are struggling with it."

"I know. I desperately need your input from your knowledge of the farm, the land and the weather conditions."

"You need help with that? Well, look over there. That's

where the farmland ends. Beyond that low ridge is the river. Here..." he sweeps his arm in an arc "...are the fields. The soil is good, the land is flat. There is one drawback, however. The ground here is subject to winter flooding – at the beginning of winter and then again during the spring thaw."

"I realize that. But when will the flooding begin?"

"The fields around here will become waterlogged soon. One heavy downpour is all it will take."

"Yes, but when?"

"It could be tomorrow. Or not for another two weeks."

"And that puts an end to gathering the crop."

"Correct. The ground will become a muddy swamp. The truck will not be able to travel – not on any boards you design."

Sergei sighs dejectedly. "And the potato crop will be rendered inaccessible. And rot in the ground."

"Yes. You are not telling me anything I don't already know." Vladimir places his hand on Sergei's shoulder and brightens up a notch. "But this is not inevitable – the loss of the crop, I mean."

"How come? You know that I have been seeking a solution. Trying to find a way to save the entire crop."

"There is a practice in parts of Russia to store root vegetables underground in winter pits. Are you familiar with it?"

"I have heard of it, but never experienced it. Truth be known, I have never experienced any farming at all."

The two men reach the low ridge. It ranges from two to three metres higher than the flat land of the fields. They walk to the crest and view the fast-moving river on the other side. Vladimir describes the landscape. "This place here, the brow of the ridge, is higher than the fields. When the fields flood, this remains dry. But not for the entire winter. You see, this ridge runs parallel to the river. It marks the highwater mark of the river during the spring thaw. The ridge is formed by multiple years of river mud left behind by the retreating water. This spot, where we are standing, will be under water in March. But the lower fields will be waterlogged for the entire winter, from November to the end of March."

"And when the frost hits, the fields will be frozen solid."

"Impossible to dig. And any crop that survives the

initial flooding will undoubtedly be destroyed by the frost."

"I get it. You recommend digging pits here on the ridge."

"Look back at the fields, Sergei. See the zeks at work gathering potatoes by hand? You can see the progress made in three days? Now picture the progress from now until the end of the month."

Sergei pictures the fields as they might appear in two weeks. Even allowing for the recent innovations, there is a limit to how much can be trucked from the fields to the farm. At the most optimistic rate of trucking, a vast area of the fields will remain untouched. "We will never succeed in harvesting the entire crop."

"I agree. At our projected rate of gathering, we will lose over half the crop."

"Surely this is of concern to the administrator. Is it not?"

"The prison administrator? His attention is focused on punishing zeks and meeting his quota. This crop that you see out there could fill his quota twice over, but it may not interest him. Sergei, I am not like him. I am not a prison administrator; I am a farm manager. I like to save my crops. If we are to save this crop, the answer lies in pits."

"Vladimir, you are a genius. Take advantage of the downtime, when the zeks perform non-productive tasks…"

"I am a jump ahead of you, Sergei. We need to redirect some of the labour to filling potato pits here on the ridge. However, to utilize zek labour, we need the administrator's authorization."

"And this is it. At last, my 'step five'. I will draw up a presentation to win over the administrator. 'Selling' is a skill I learned in America. If he believes that it will enhance his performance record, and positions him for a promotion, he will support it."

"And in the meantime, I will direct the guards to have idle zeks dig pits as an apt activity for downtime."

They return to the field of activity. Vladimir speaks with the guard in charge. The guard is from a peasant family and knows how to winterize root crops in underground pits. He agrees to engage the zeks in digging pits during otherwise idle periods. He considers digging to be harsher punishment for idle zeks than walking in circles, and much more satisfying.

Sergei and Vladimir return to the farm. At the service garage, Vladimir puts the finishing touches to the second trailer. The trailers are fragile. He hopes that they will survive ten trips to and from the railway siding. He warns the men to be careful when driving over bumps, or when rounding a corner, or when travelling up a hill, or down a hill. Fortunately, the trip to the railway siding is mostly on a straight road on level ground. The greatest hazard, however, might be from an inquisitive member of the politsiya inspecting a trailer for roadworthiness. As a final touch, Vladimir fixes old cart lamps to the rear of the trailers to serve as taillights.

Late in the evening, as night is falling, two fully-laden lorries, driven by Pyotr and Gregori, depart on an overnight journey to the railway station. Three-and-a-half truckloads remain in the storage barn, ready for loading onto lorries on the following day. Sergei is pleased with the progress. He is ready to present the final stages of the five-step plan to the administrator – boxes and pits.

That same evening, the administrator requests the farm manager to attend in his office for the daily report. He also asks for Sergei to attend. He now refers to Sergei as an 'innovator', but still a lowly zek. Vladimir updates the administrator on the success of the trailers fitted to the lorries. Denis is pleased to learn that, as of tomorrow, the labour farm will deliver three lorryloads of potatoes to the railcars daily. But this will slow to two-and-a-half loads daily when the stored crop is exhausted. The daily output from the fields is 10 farm-truck loads, equalling two-and-a-half lorryloads. And, if the weather holds, five railcars will be filled by the deadline, with two truckloads retained in storage.

Denis, the administrator, picks up on 'if the weather holds'. His feeling of elation wanes. "What do you mean by 'if the weather holds'?" The question is directed at the farm manager.

Vladimir enlightens him. "Once the fields become swamped by the winter rains, harvesting will cease. The truck will unable to navigate through the waterlogged land to the fields. And digging in muddy water will be futile."

"And when will this happen?"

"The rains have already started. But so far, only light showers. Nevertheless, every day becomes wetter and muddier. Traditionally, the fields become unworkable in the first week of November."

"The first week of November is after our deadline.

We'll have the railcars filled by then – five railcars."

"Comrade Lieutenant, I said **'if'**. One deluge of rain would render the fields waterlogged. And that could happen any time within the next two weeks, perhaps even in two days. We don't know."

"I see. This is not good news. So, we are in a race against the weather?"

"That's right. However, there is a workaround. First, let Sergei present the final steps of his plan. Then we can evaluate the most favourable option."

Denis raises his eyebrows at Sergei to indicate to him to proceed. Sergei, 'the innovator', hands sheets of paper to the two men. He proceeds to explain his plan.

"First, step number four. It is documented on page one. Elevated loading boxes – erected at the digging location in the fields. As of tomorrow, the truck will henceforth be loaded from boxes pre-filled by the zeks. Loading will take less than one minute. This shortens the truck's turnaround time and enables it to complete four round trips per day instead of the current three." Sergei pauses. He looks up at the picture of the smiling Stalin and hopes that it is a smile of approval. He resumes his presentation. "Now to step number five. It's on the following page. Note that it refers back to step number four as it pertains to the zeks filling the elevated boxes. Currently, we have 76 zeks…"

"We have 77, Comrade Innovator. Don't forget that you are still a zek. And you will be back at physical labour once your ideas are fully implemented."

"My apologies, Comrade Administrator. Currently, we have 77 zeks, of which one is working as an innovator, 12 as zek runners, and 64 as zek labourers in the fields. The truck turning point is located close to the digging – it always is. That's due to the mobility of the turning platform and the elevated boxes. Twenty zeks can fill the boxes in preparation for the truck. That leaves 44 zeks for working the pits."

"The pits?"

"Let me finish. We currently transport potatoes from the fields to the farm at the rate of 10 truckloads per day. Bear in mind, the zeks can excavate potatoes at a faster rate than the truck can carry. However, we can place additional potatoes in underground winter storage in the high ground by the river. This is an area that remains free of flooding until March. Look at the diagrams on page three. It gives the dimensions of the pits. The interior of each pit will be insulated with dry straw. And it will be filled with alternating layers of potatoes, dirt and straw. Note the thatched exposed exterior, like a rooftop, to permit water runoff. And notice how the pits are angled relative to the slope to permit drainage. These pits are dry and frost-free, perfect for winter storage. So, when the truck is no longer able to transport the crop back to the farm, the remainder of the potatoes will be safe in the winter pits. Just consider the number of potatoes 44 zeks can place into pits."

"A lot more than what is trucked back to the farm. I see. But what happens in March? Will not the high ground and the pits be flooded by then?"

"No. The pits will be excavated and emptied in December when the frost arrives. And the contents will be safely stored in the storage barns."

"In December? There is one drawback to your plan. We will have passed the deadline in December – too late to fulfill our quota requirements."

"But not if a second deadline is granted for a second 'harvest'. We are talking about an additional five railcar loads – a rich bonus. Don't you think that the ministry would be pleased with that?"

Denis Novak is deep in thought. This is too good for the

ministry to ignore. And it could garner him his desired promotion. A few days ago, he was toying with his gun and contemplating death. Back then, the chances of filling one railcar were slim. The quota of six carloads appeared unattainable. Tonight, he was satisfied that he could reach an acceptable five carloads. Suddenly, he is presented with 10 carloads. Even if the weather turns bad and he fails to fill five railcars by the deadline, he can still deliver 10 loads in total – provided he is granted an extension. He wonders if the ministry will agree to late delivery. If they are desperate for potatoes for export, how could they reject his request? The administrator decides that there is only one way to find out – contact the ministry.

"Comrade Lieutenant, do we have your authorization to proceed with step number five?" Vladimir brings his attention back to the meeting.

Denis looks up at him and says, "Proceed as the zek innovator proposes. Now, go to it. The meeting is over."

Vladimir and Sergei leave the administrator's office. Denis starts to compose a detailed report to the ministry. He hopes to impress them with the innovations he implemented which will result in exceeding the quota by 67%. And he requests two deadlines – the original five railcars loaded by 31

October, and five additional railcars loaded by 31 December.

CHAPTER NINE

POTATOES FOR MOSCOW

The days pass with ever-increasing anxiety. The camp administrator fears that he may fall short of securing five fully-loaded railcars by the deadline. To fill five railcars out of a required quota of six will likely render him a 'pass' and a mild reprimand. Anything less could be detrimental to his career. Day after day, he pushes the field labourers to exhaustion. To supplement what is transported by the farm truck, the weary zeks are forced to carry creels of potatoes on their return journeys from the fields at the end of each day. To assist them in maintaining a secure footing on the muddy ground, they are provided with walking staffs. Due to deteriorating ground conditions, the route taken by the farm truck becomes deeply rutted. The truck is forced to carry lighter loads and alter its route daily. Two weeks earlier, the projected achievable target was expected to fill five railcars and retain a surplus of two truckloads for the farm. Today, the rainfall is heavy. It severely hampers the work. And it appears that there will be a disastrous shortfall by an estimated two truckloads. The ground has become so soft from the rains that, by mid-morning, the farm truck is no longer able to navigate any workable route to the potato fields. With two days to the deadline, Denis Novak presses Sergei and Vladimir to come up with a solution. Failing a promising input from the zek innovator, Sergei will be relegated back to carrying potatoes in a creel.

On the final day, they delay the departure of the transport lorry to midday. Any later, and it will not reach the rail siding in time. Vladimir draws up the bill of lading and gives it to Boris who is entrusted with the delivery. At midday, it departs with half a load. As the lorry exits the yard, Boris reads the bill of lading for the train – a shipment of potatoes totalling four full railcars plus 80% of a railcar.

Meanwhile, Sergei has an idea, inspired by desperation rather than genius. He presents it to Vladimir, who jumps into action. The farm manager enlists the prison staff and sends them to the fields to join the group of zek labourers. They are instructed to carry potatoes back to the farm in creels, bags, sacks and even blankets. He has no authority to order this. But the entire camp is aware of the urgency of the situation. When Denis Novak learns of this, he summons Sergei and Vladimir to explain.

In the administrator's office, Sergei speaks forcefully. "Comrade Lieutenant, look around you. There are zeks, prison staff, guards, farmworkers and a camp administrator. And what do we have in common? First and foremost, we are workers. We are at our most efficient when we coordinate our efforts. We are strongest when united."

Denis smarts at the lecturing tone of the zek. He is about to order a punishment but bites his tongue. The unauthorized action taken by these two men is justifiable under the circumstances. He glances at the bust of Lenin on the shelf above the door and reads the motto underneath, 'WORKERS OF THE WORLD UNITE'. When he eventually speaks, Denis utters, "Workers of Corrective Farm No.47 unite. You have my authorization to proceed as you see fit. But next time, inform me **before** you act. Dismissed!"

Later, alone in his office, Denis is struck by the sentiment uttered so strongly by the zek – 'We are workers, strongest when united'. He opens his desk drawer and removes a file. Next to the name 'Sergei Falkov' he writes 'Rehabilitation promising'.

Upon entering the yard, Vladimir enlists Gregori to drive the farm truck to the collective farm at Bichurga-Baishevo, 25 kilometres away, and obtain a load of potatoes from their harvested stock. He instructs him to sequester or commandeer the potatoes if necessary.

Gregori is taken aback. "What? You want me to steal a truckload of potatoes from the neighbouring farm? It's their food."

Vladimir is impatient. "Use gentle persuasion, in the spirit of cooperation. And remind them that they graze a herd of cattle here. Take a prison guard with you, one with an intimidating rifle."

"As you order. But it is still stealing."

"No, Gregori. It is borrowing. We will repay them in three days with a return load. No. We will insert side panels on the truck – a load-and-a-half. Tell them that. Now, get going."

Throughout the remainder of the day, small loads of potatoes trickle in from the fields. The contents of each basket, bag and receptacle are tipped into the designated lorry.

An hour and a half after departing from the yard, Gregori returns. He has succeeded in obtaining a full load of potatoes. He also gained an unexpected passenger. Olga Abramchenko, the manager of the collective farm, disembarks and makes straight for Vladimir. She is furious at the farm manager's highhanded action and demands an explanation. The truckload of potatoes represents their winter stock of food, without which they will go hungry. Vladimir quickly appeases her. He briefly explains his dilemma with the quota deadline. He directs her attention to the incoming potatoes that workers are bringing in from the fields. She sizes up the activity and realizes that the labour farm has sufficient potatoes to replenish a truckload, but at the rate of gathering, perhaps not for a few days. She reminds Vladimir of his promise to repay the load with a 50% bonus.

Olga's potatoes are loaded into the lorry – it is late in the day. Vladimir perceives that the cargo reaches the halfway level. Thereupon, he enters his office and hastily draws up a new waybill. He takes it and a bulky envelope and tosses them into the cab of the lorry. Next, he grabs a greatcoat from the service garage and tosses it to Sergei. "Come on!" he shouts. "You are coming with me to Zelenyj Dol Station."

Sergei, lugging the greatcoat in his arms, climbs into the passenger side of the lorry. Before he has time to settle or shut the door, Vladimir accelerates out of the yard. The lorry kicks up dirt and mud as the skidding wheels struggle for traction. One fishtail later, the truck is speeding on its way to the railway station.

Sergei settles into his seat. He considers that the truck is proceeding at the speed of folly. Subconsciously, he presses his foot on an imaginary brake. When he has recovered, he speaks to Vladimir. "How long will this take – the journey to the rail siding? And why am I here, anyway?"

Vladimir is intent on keeping his eyes on the road and his mind on the driving. He changes gears until he reaches cruising speed. Then, he responds. "In daylight, in good conditions, the trip takes nine hours. But this will take longer. You understand that this is an overnight journey. There is intermittent rain and the road surface is slick. We will not reach the railway station until tomorrow. But the train departs at noon. I need your American skill of 'selling' to have the stationmaster permit us to load our cargo prior to departure – if we arrive in adequate time."

"So, why the greatcoat?"

"Huh! Do you think the stationmaster will listen to a zek? He would have you shot. This will not happen, Sergei. Today, you are an administrator. So, try to look the part."

This worries Sergei. If he is exposed, both of them will be shot.

Night falls. Because of the absence of road markings, Vladimir has difficulty distinguishing the margin of the road. They encounter drizzle and patches of fog. After a few hours, Sergei falls asleep. Later, he is jolted awake. The lorry has come to an abrupt halt. At first, he thinks they have reached their destination, but it cannot be so – it is still night. He peers out through the wet dirt-smeared windshield and beholds a heap of gravel and a looming rock face illuminated by the lights of the lorry.

Sergei turns to Vladimir and asks, "Where the hell are we?"

Vladimir stares ahead with the engine running. "It can't be a dead end. I frequently drive this route." He steps out from the lorry to view the surroundings in the lights of the lorry. He returns to the cab and laughs in relief. "I missed a turn back there. I've driven into a roadside quarry that stores gravel for road repairs. I know where I am now. Step outside, Sergei, and direct me as I reverse back to the roadway."

Sergei obliges. Moments later, they resume their journey. After the near-mishap, Vladimir drives with increased caution. Whenever he drives through a patch of fog, he rolls down his window to listen to the sound of the tires. The gravel surface is coarser at the edge of the roadway. If he hears a crunching sound from the tires, he knows that he has strayed from the centre of the road. Later, when daylight breaks, the weather dries.

Vladimir increases speed.

At mid-morning, they arrive at the rail siding. But the railcars are gone. They conclude that the cars have already been shunted. Vladimir sees a train parked alongside a platform in the station. It is on the other side of the tracks, ten sets of tracks away, in the distance. He reasons that this is the train carrying the potato railcars. It is necessary to drive the lorry back to the roadway, cross a bridge, and approach the station from the opposite side. Alas, the platform is not accessible to the lorry. Vladimir parks as close as possible to the front of the building. Thereupon, the two men stride to the railway office. Sergei fastens his greatcoat at his throat to conceal his zek work clothes. In the office, Sergei adopts an 'important voice' and has Vladimir present a modified bill of lading for the potato consignment. The clerk refers to a sheaf of waybills on his desk. He locates the documents pertaining to the five railcars of potatoes. He informs them that the goods have not yet left the station and that they are on the train ready to depart. However, to alter the load at this late stage is irregular and he would need the approval of the stationmaster.

Sergei turns to Vladimir and says, "Sergeant, go to the Post and Telegraph office and send a message to the ministry. Inform them that we have successfully delivered the cargo as requested." He turns to face the clerk but continues speaking to Vladimir. "Shipment will be executed today – unless the railway staff thinks otherwise."

The nervous clerk summons the stationmaster. The stationmaster is very busy. He answers impatiently. "You wish to increase your cargo to a full-capacity load? The train leaves in one hour and ten minutes. All cargo must be secured with proper documents lodged a half-hour before departure." He glances disapprovingly at the mud-smeared documents tendered by Vladimir. However, they appear to bear official stamps in indelible ink. He says to the clerk, "See to it. Modified cargo to be loaded and secured by 11:30." The stationmaster marches off, leaving the problem in the hands of an anxious clerk.

The clerk addresses Sergei. "The stationmaster approves. Proceed to load your remaining cargo in railcar number BX4204. It is the fifth from the front."

"Thank you, Comrade. Now, we need to transfer the remaining cargo from our lorry to the railcar. The lorry is parked out front since it has no access to the platform."

The clerk returns a puzzled look. This is an added

problem.

Sergei jolts the clerk into action. "You have porters, yes? And porters have handcarts, yes? So, summon sufficient porters to transfer the goods."

The clerk runs out to the platform and blows his whistle. He assembles a group of porters and instructs them to be of service to the 'army administrator'.

At 11:30, Sergei and Vladimir stand on the platform and congratulate each other. Five railcars are fully loaded and secured, ready for shipment to Moscow. In the station office, the guard (conductor) from the train obtains copies of waybills and consignment notes and all documentation relevant to the train's cargo. Next, he walks to the Post and Telegraph office and picks up a postbag. Thus laden, he enters the guard's van, the caboose at the rear of the train. The railway staff conducts a visual check of each railcar. When satisfied, each man steps back exactly two metres. The guard flips coloured paddles at the side of the guard's van to communicate the 'all clear' to the engineer. The stationmaster walks along the row of men, like a general passing a guard of honour. He stops at the locomotive, consults his watch, and passes the baton to the engineer. With the passing of the baton, the train leaves the charge of the stationmaster and transfers to the engineer. The engine blows steam and expels smoke and the train inches forward. Each car jolts slightly as the couplings clunk with tension. The clunking sound runs along the train from car to car. In the silence that follows, the train appears to be motionless. However, it is slowly moving imperceptibly. Then, the squeak of a wheel, the creak of a swaying car, and the train increases speed. By the time it clears the platform, it is travelling at cantering speed. Sergei and Vladimir remain on the platform until the train disappears from view. The distant smoke is still distinguishable as they turn away.

Sergei speaks aloud to himself. "We did it. Five fully-laden railcars of potatoes going to Moscow. And who knows where after that. Germany, perhaps?"

Vladimir turns to face him and says, "We are not yet finished." He walks to the Post and Telegraph office and sends a message to the ministry to report that the shipment has departed Zelenodolsk. Next, he walks back to the lorry and retrieves the large envelope from the cab. He waves it at Sergei. "This," he says, "is the report from the camp administrator. It was completed a week ago. I was instructed to post it only if, and when, the goods were successfully dispatched. So, now I post it."

"And if we had failed to load the remaining cargo?"

"I would return it to Administrator Denis Novak. He would compose a new report – or maybe not."

After posting the envelope, Sergei says with much relief, "It is done, completed, mission accomplished."

"A-ha! There is one last task. Let's go to the railway canteen and eat some borscht. We will set out to the farm in 15 minutes."

Later, in the canteen, Sergei chews vigorously on chunks of tough meat. It has a delightful taste, but his jaw aches. "Vladimir, this is going to take more than 15 minutes."

On the journey back, Sergei experiences a coziness that is denied to a zek. He falls asleep.

CHAPTER TEN

THE INSPECTOR AND THE INNOVATOR

November enters with an invasion of heavy rain clouds. The zek workers are no longer able to traverse through the muddy ground to the potato fields. Some sections of the ground are knee-deep in mud. Vladimir, however, finds an alternative passageway. He leads the zeks to the potato fields by walking over the grassy tufts of the grazing lands to the river and thence along the riverbank. It takes four hours to reach the pits by the new route. The accompanying guards leave the leadership of the work detail in the hands of the farm manager. Vladimir determines that today, 03 November, is the last day to attempt the journey. He directs the day's final tasks. The entire crop is effectively harvested. The potatoes have either been transported to the farm or are deposited safely in pits. He conducts final thatching of the roof-shaped surfaces of the pits. He is satisfied that the pits are insulated from frost and are adequately waterproofed. He directs the zeks to dismantle the loading boxes and the turning platform. There is a bunch of straw under a waterproof cover – the leftover insulation straw. He has the zeks carry the dismantled boxes, the planks from the platform and the canvas cover, back to the farm. He leaves the surplus straw behind. There is a plentiful supply of straw in storage at the farm, the by-product of the earlier oat harvest. In the course of the 10-hour day, less than two hours are dedicated to the actual work in the fields. When they reach the farm, at the end of an exacting day, the zeks and guards and Vladimir are caked in sticky mud to the knees. And their entire bodies are soaked in splatter. Without exception, every man is wet and cold. The guards order the zeks into the bathhouse to strip and wash and obtain dry clothes. The guards themselves undergo the same ritual. For a brief time, mud renders the zeks and guards as equals.

On the same day, Gregori is particularly active. Ever since he commandeered a load of potatoes from the neighbouring collective farm, he has been remorseful. Vladimir is focused on the deteriorating work conditions in the potato fields and appears to have forgotten his commitment to repay the potato debt. Not so, Gregori. He loads the farm truck with potatoes from storage. By inserting the extension panels, he achieves a load-and-a-half. When he is finished, less than a truckload of potatoes remains behind in the barn. This does not deter him. The administrator is unable to observe him from the prison building. And Vladimir is off in the distant fields. There is no one around to order him to desist. He cautiously exits the farmyard and executes the delivery. Later, if he is challenged by Vladimir, he can plead that there was an implied order resulting from the original pledge.

At the end of the day, Vladimir is changing out of his muddy clothing in the service garage. He summons Gregori. Gregori enters with fingers crossed. Vladimir is buttoning his tunic. Without turning around to face him, Vladimir says, "Don't forget to bring a load of potatoes to Bichurga-Baishevo. It's their winter food requirements, you know."

Gregori is relieved. Yet, he wonders if the wily manager knows. "At once. Oh, is it not a load-and-a-half?"

"So, it is. I trust you to see to it promptly, Gregori. After all, the farm manager has faith in his loyal workers."

Gregori frets to himself, "Damn, he already knows."

Later, at the daily meeting, the administrator is relieved, but still unhappy. He is relieved that the rail cargo of potatoes is safely on its way. Nonetheless, he remains anxious regarding his failure to meet his assigned quota. The report he sent ought to explain the situation to the satisfaction of the 'clowns' in Moscow. Furthermore, the promise of an additional cargo should earn him a reprieve – or a promotion. The report was posted on Thursday. Someone must have read it by now. Vladimir tenders his daily report and updates him on winterizing the farm. The crops are secure in the pits; the storage barn contains adequate potatoes for their needs. In addition, there is an ample supply of cabbage and dried fish. Storage barns and unheated buildings are being insulated with straw. Vladimir continues with his list. Much of the information is foreign to Denis. He ceases listening, satisfied that the farm manager has things in hand.

Suddenly, Denis interrupts the manager's presentation. "Tomorrow, the zeks will rest. And they will be given double portions of food. Thanks for your report, Comrade Kotyakov. You are dismissed." And with that, the baffled farm manager leaves the office.

On the following day, a car arrives at the labour camp. It is a surprise visit by an inspector from the Ministry of the Interior, Corrective Labour Camps Division. He is ushered, with immense fuss, to the administrator's office. He enters hastily with authority.

Denis stands to attention and says, "Welcome, Comrade. I am Lieutenant-Administrator Denis Novak."

"And I am Alexander Matytsin, an inspector for the ministry."

"Yes, of course. Please be seated. I am at your service." The inspector sits and Denis also.

The inspector casts his eyes around the office. It appears neat and orderly. And the smiling picture of Stalin meets with his approval. He notices the bust of Lenin and the motto of the Soviet Republic. He comes to the point of his visit. "Comrade Lieutenant, we received your report yesterday. It contains a few unexpected items that caught our interest."

Denis calculates the driving time from Moscow. It takes 15 hours by car. The inspector would have travelled through the night. He wonders what warrants an inspection so soon. This does not bode well. He hopes that his report was favourably received. "Yes, Comrade Inspector?" He waits for the inspector to continue.

"We are interested in the 'pontoon-boards'. You state that this innovation was responsible for saving your harvest. Of course, you shipped only five full railcars of potatoes, when your quota was six. So, not quite a success. Let's say, this innovation averted a catastrophe."

Lieutenant Denis Novak is braced for a scathing reprimand. "Comrade, we have harvested twice that amount. The crop is safely stored in winterized pits in…"

"Pontoon-boards! I am talking about pontoon-boards. What are they? What do they do, exactly? Your report identified a zek labourer as the person responsible, one named Sergei Falkov. Is this true?"

Lieutenant Novak is somewhat relieved. The urgent matter that brings the inspector here so quickly pertains to the pontoon-boards. "Yes, Comrade Inspector. The pontoon-boards. The idea came from a zek worker, Sergei Falkov. He was an inventor at one time. He has presented us with several innovations in our labour camp."

"Bring me Sergei Falkov. I would like to know about this 'pontoon-board' that saved your harvest."

Denis remembers that he has given the zeks a day of rest. Sergei Falkov cannot be far away, at least not out in the potato fields, a four-hour walk away. He calls the junior guard from the adjoining office and instructs him to bring Sergei Falkov. The prison guards are aware of the presence of the inspector and have assembled the zeks for an anticipated inspection. Sergei is located within minutes and is ushered into the administrator's office.

Sergei stands to attention. The inspector scrutinizes him closely. His work clothes are unexpectedly clean. His facial hair is long and unkempt. He is of a weak build, unsuited to the physical labour demanded of a zek. Zeks like this are literally worked to death within a year.

Alexander addresses him. "You are Sergei Falkov?"

"Yes, Comrade."

The inspector is surprised at the voice. It is strong and confident with no hint of meekness. It betrays an attitude inappropriate for a zek. He continues. "And you are an inventor?"

"Was an inventor. Now I am a zek."

"But you invented something here in the camp, did you not?"

"I help the work by offering innovations."

"Are not inventions and innovations the same?"

"Sometimes. Innovation is putting an invention to work. Or it could be a new way of doing something old. It is practical rather than theoretical."

"So, you present new practical ways?"

"To help with the work, yes."

"Ways to help with the work," he echoes. "Explain 'pontoon-board'."

"Comrade Inspector, an explanation is lengthy, but a demonstration is self-explanatory and precise. And is more accurate than a verbal explanation. There are pontoon-boards in the service garage which have endured punishing treatment – and survived undamaged."

Alexander regards Sergei's bold statement. Zeks are usually punished for being outspoken. In this instance, the inspector is curious and lets it pass. "Then, lead me to the service garage for a practical demonstration."

In the garage, Sergei shows him the pontoon-boards. He describes the need for strength – strong enough to bear the weight of a vehicle, yet sufficiently light to be lifted with little physical effort. Sergei asks a bold question. "Comrade Inspector, I see you came here in a car. Did you experience muddy conditions on your trip here?"

"I drove in the centre of the road on the approach to the farm. It would be hazardous to venture close to the edge."

"And if you drive onto the shoulder?"

"The car would bog down in the soft ground."

"Then let's try it using the boards."

"Are you inviting me to drive my car onto the shoulder with just these boards to prevent me from sinking?"

The farm manager smiles and reassures the inspector that the boards have been used successfully for heavier vehicles. "Don't worry. Your car will be safe."

Alexander Matytsin considers that this might be a trick to embarrass him. Then again, who would dare play a trick on a ministry inspector? If they did, he would have them all shot and the camp administrator would be relegated to a labour camp as a zek within a week. On the other hand, he must not appear timid. If for no other reason than to save face, the inspector agrees to the challenge. Vladimir requests the guards to fetch six zeks to act as runners. Instead, the farm staff and two guards volunteer for the demonstration.

Minutes later, Alexander is driving his car on the farm's access road. Vladimir communicates to him with hand gestures. The inspector drives the car to the margin; the two left wheels mount the boards. But there is no sensation of sinking. Thus emboldened, he drives farther until all four wheels are on what should be boggy mud. But the boards support the car effortlessly. After 50 metres, he drives back onto the solid roadway. Next, Vladimir arranges the boards in a rectangle to provide a turning point. Alexander executes a three-point turn and returns to the farmyard. He is impressed. To maintain dignity, he struggles to hide his excitement. But the glow in his eyes betrays him.

Back in the service garage, Alexander requests a sample board with relevant drawings of specifications. Sergei enters the farm manager's office and selects a file from a cabinet. He hands a copy of the requested documents to the inspector.

The inspector accepts the documents from the zek and raises his eyebrows. "You have an office?"

Vladimir tenders an explanation. "It's my office. I let Sergei use it when he is working on designs. Where else, but here? As you see, the office has all the paraphernalia for drawing, measuring and sketching ideas; the service garage has all the necessary carpentry tools and machine tools. When an idea is ready for development, Sergei presents it to me. If I approve, the farm staff work on building a prototype."

"The zek has an office **and** staff at his service?" This is more than the inspector has encountered in any labour camp.

Vladimir continues with his explanation. "He is currently designing a 'To/Fro hinge' for the main gates. And a roller for lorry covers."

"What do you mean by a 'roller for lorry covers'?"

Sergei interrupts. "The cargo of a lorry needs protection from the weather. To cover and uncover the bed, two men are required to stretch and tug the canvas into position. But if the tarpaulin is rolled, instead of folded, it can be moved on a roller by a single person. It is the same principle as a window blind. All it needs is a well-designed roller and two cords on pulleys. It is a quick operation and fits snugly. Well, it will be when the design is perfected and executed."

Alexander is taking note of this. The unorthodox behaviour of the zek warrants severe punishment. And the prison and farm staff are complicit. Yet, in an inverted way, it seems right. The inspector is deep in thought. After a moment he speaks. "You mentioned a 'To/Fro hinge'."

Vladimir responds. "Yes. After all, Sergei is the inventor."

Alexander turns to the zek. "Your name is Sergei

Falkov?" He asks this as if the name holds some significance.

"Yes."

Alexander Matytsin thinks back to 1922 when Lenin's government introduced the New Economic Policy which resulted in a period of economic recovery. During this period, Russian innovation was encouraged. He remembers that he once attended a demonstration of the 'To/Fro Balanced Hinge'. As was the policy, and still is, all inventions are presented as 'Russian inventions' or 'Army inventions' or inventions originating at a particular ministry. The actual inventor is never identified. However, it was accepted that the demonstration of the 'To/Fro Balanced Hinge' was conducted by the inventor himself. Alexander remembers the name of the presenter at the demonstration he witnessed – 'Falkov'. It dawns on him that the zek now standing before him is the inventor of the 'To/Fro Balanced Hinge', a man once respected in Russia. He addresses the men in the service garage. "Comrades, I have seen enough." He takes his sample pontoon-board and the drawing. He returns to the administrator's office.

Back in Lieutenant Novak's office, the inspector moves on to the next item of attention. "You say that you have saved a crop of potatoes equal to five railcars. That is, in addition to the five cars already shipped. And that the crop is safely stored in pits. Is this correct?"

"Yes, Comrade Inspector."

"Then, show me. Take me to the pits to see for myself."

"I'm sorry, Comrade Inspector. The pits are five kilometres from here. The only way to reach them is across water-logged fields. What I mean is, the pits are inaccessible until the frost arrives. To travel there, we must wait for the ground to freeze."

"So, let me understand. You have a crop of potatoes saved, but you cannot show me?"

"That's right."

Alexander semi-shuts his eyes and stares ominously at the administrator. "I inspect many labour camps. And I hear many stories. There is one story I would like to impart to you. You know, some administrators lie about their harvests. When they fall short of their quota, they inflate their figures to make it appear otherwise. Then, they blame some outside event for the 'unexpected loss' – a fire, a flood, theft and so forth. They attempt to have the record show that they achieved their quota, when in fact they failed. Could this be the case here?"

"No, Comrade. Of course not. I can show you figures…"

"And then there is the other story. An administrator under-reports the actual yield so that he can conceal some of the crop and later sell it on the black market. Now, Comrade Administrator, let's say I don't believe that you have a substantial crop saved in some inaccessible place. The record would show that your entire crop is accounted for – a harvest that fell short of the required quota. And the hidden crop could then be diverted to the black market."

"But, but…"

"But in your situation, I challenge you to stand by your claim. You will transport an additional five full railcars of potatoes by 31 December. By that time, the ground should be sufficiently hardened by frost. So, you will have no trouble meeting the increased quota. Will you?"

Denis swallows. There is no negotiating. This is a demand. "Yes, Comrade Inspector."

"Now for the final matter. The prison will be vacated as of the 7th of November. The guards, the prison staff and the zeks will be removed. The prison employees will be relocated. Those who were serving light sentences will be released. The zeks are part of a mobile workforce. They will be moved to other labour camps."

"Comrade Inspector, I need workers for the final shipment of potatoes."

"Ah, yes. So, you do. I will leave you two guards and 10 zeks. That ought to be adequate to load the remaining potatoes. Don't forget, the permanent farm staff remains with the farm. They are not prison personnel; they are answerable to the Ministry of Agriculture. That's five additional workers for your potatoes. Bear in mind, the ministry may not agree with my recommendation. The 10 zeks are yours until the end of December, or until they are needed at another labour camp."

Denis knows that it is unwise to argue. "Yes, Comrade. That will be fine. May I choose the 10 zeks that will remain?"

"Comrade Administrator, I will choose which zeks will remain behind. Show me your register." Denis draws the register from his desk and hands it to the inspector.

Alexander goes through the list of zeks and chooses the 10 oldest. In doing so, he notices the remark written beside the name Sergei Falkov – 'REHABILITATION PROMISING'. Alexander quizzes the administrator on the entry.

Denis relates to him the incident in which Sergei recommended that prison employees and guards should engage in physical labour alongside the zeks. It occurred on the day of the deadline for the quota when the weather conditions were harsh. "I remember what he said at the time. 'First and foremost, we are workers. We are at our most efficient when we coordinate our efforts. We are strongest when united.'"

"And what was your response?"

"Workers of Corrective Farm No.47 unite."

"Indeed." Alexander Matytsin has an interesting report to file. He conducts a quick tour of the prison. Having concluded his inspection, he departs, taking the sample pontoon-board and relevant drawings.

In his office, Denis Novak feels that the inspection went well. He pats his gun holster and says, "Not today. But some other day, who knows what curve the future will throw?"

CHAPTER ELEVEN

WINTER ON THE FARM

It is 06 November. Lieutenant-Administrator Denis Novak completes the forms for the transfer of zeks and prison staff. Tomorrow, the surplus body of workers, staff and guards will be transferred to the Ministry of the Interior, Corrective Labour Camps Division, for re-assignment or release. The prison staff perform their final duties in preparation for vacating the building. Some of the zeks are employed in winterizing the farm – repairing and insulating the storage stalls in the barns. Sergeant-Manager Vladimir Kotyakov supervises work on the farm. During the winter, the lorries and farm truck will be kept in the service garage when not on the road. He ensures that the garage windows are covered with sacking to protect against the invading winter frost. The downside to this is that no light enters the garage except through the open doors. Otherwise, interior lighting is required. There is one electric light in the building – not enough to be of much use. The generator is utilized on an as-need basis for limited periods during the day, and never after lights-out. Oil lamps, of which there is a plentiful supply, are the preferred source of lighting.

On the following day, army lorries arrive at the labour camp. The transfer is executed promptly. Thereupon, the lorries depart. Denis watches the lorries leave through the compound gates and onto the mud-splattered access road and out of sight. Two guards and 10 zeks remain behind. With only two guards, the administrator is unable to man the four watchtowers or provide full prison security. However, how difficult is it to guard 10 zeks? Provided they are confined together as a single unit, they are unlikely to attempt an escape. To keep them occupied, Denis orders the zeks to undertake mundane duties – water-cart duties, latrine duties, scrubbing floors, washing walls, cleaning windows and numerous fatigue duties.

Sergei Falkov is occupied in the service garage and is exempted from the mundane tasks imposed upon the other zeks. Throughout November, he designs To/Fro Balanced Hinges which the farmworkers build and thereafter install on the main gate of the compound. Once a week, a farmworker drives to Zelenyj Dol Station to check the post and obtain supplies. At the main gate to the farmyard, the driver can now open and shut the gate from the comfort of his cab as he enters or leaves the yard. Previously, a guard was posted as gatekeeper. The farm also benefits from other innovations. The two transport lorries and the farm truck are outfitted with roll-away canvas covers.

Gregori makes frequent trips to the Bichurga-Baishevo

Collective Farm, where he has formed a friendship with Olga, the collective's manager. On several occasions, he brings Sergei to the collective to implement his innovations there. The To/Fro Balanced Hinges are effectively installed. The collective rewards them with goose eggs and duck eggs and jars of preserves. Back in the service garage, the farmworkers enjoy a superior diet to the prison fare. They include Sergei in the feasting, but keep their newfound fortune a secret from the prison administrator.

Over the weeks, Sergei feels at home in the service garage. He still sleeps in the zek dormitory, but otherwise, he is employed on the farm under the supervision of the farm manager. He is free to move about in the garage. He works on his designs and eats with his personal utensils. He is privileged to have access to the farm's brick outhouse. It is an outhouse because it is outside. But it abuts the service garage and is accessed through a hatch from the garage. The primary rule in using the outhouse is to have the hatch fully closed at all times. This prevents unwelcome odours from entering the garage but, more importantly, it keeps the annoying flies out.

One day, after enjoying an oversized fried goose egg, Sergei starts on a plan to make the farm self-sufficient in food. There is an existing relationship with the collective. It would be a small step to acquire live ducklings and goslings from them. And, in the spirit of cooperation, zek labour could be shared with the collective at critical periods. The project could expand to include one or two milk cows and, in time, alleviate the expense of shipping in food for the prison. The proposal, if accepted, would require the coordination of both ministries – the Ministry of Agriculture and the Corrective Labour Camps Division of the Ministry of the Interior. Cooperation between the two ministries could prove to be the greatest hurdle.

On his weekly visit to Zelenyj Dol Station, on 02 December, Vladimir learns that five railcars are placed on a siding in preparation for the shipment of potatoes. He arranges a suitable schedule for deliveries. Railway workers will be on hand to load the railcars between seven in the morning and nine at night. The workers are skilled in managing all aspects of railcar loading and maintenance. This includes lining the cars with protective straw. However, the labour camp must provide an adequate supply of insulation. He returns to the labour camp with the weekly post and supplies. On the following week, on 09 December, Vladimir delivers a load of straw. When the first load of potatoes arrives, the railcars will be prepared.

Days pass. Snow falls. The frost arrives. Vladimir goes

out each morning before daybreak and drives a pickaxe into the ground. On 14 December, the outside temperature is -15°. On this occasion, he announces that the ground is frozen to a depth of seven-and-a-half centimetres and is sufficiently solid to bear the weight of a fully-loaded farm truck. He informs the administrator. Denis Novak immediately issues orders of primary importance. As of now, the entire manpower will focus on excavating the pits and bringing the remaining potatoes to the farm where the lorries will transport the crop to the railway siding at Zelenyj Dol Station. All hands will work on this regardless of status – farmworkers, guards and zeks. He has 17 days to fill his quota. This time he cannot afford to fall short. His career depends on it.

At 8:00 am, Vladimir organizes the work crews. One guard and 10 zeks will work the pits in the fields; one guard and two farmworkers will remain at the farm to unload the truck and transfer the potatoes to the lorries or the storage barn; two farmworkers will drive the lorries to the rail siding and one will drive the farm truck to and from the fields. Vladimir includes himself as a farmworker in the work roster. Everyone understands that this is a challenge. They are left in no doubt that failure to achieve the quota will result in punitive measures – and the guards are not exempt. The distant image of a zek dying from gruelling work suddenly becomes a real prospect.

The zeks are ordered to dress in outdoor winter clothing. They are prodded to greater haste by the guards. Sergei finds himself thrust into the work unit unceremoniously. His period of service-garage privilege comes to an abrupt end. He is instructed to take a creel from the stack in the yard. He is handed a pick and shovel. And he is rudely shoved onto the bed of the farm truck with the other zeks and one guard. Vladimir tosses wads of straw into the bed. The straw lands on the zeks. "Straw for insulation!" he shouts. "It's for the trip back. To protect the potatoes from freezing."

The truck, driven by Vladimir, leaves the compound and travels over the snow-encrusted surface. The snow is five centimetres deep. The ground beneath is rough but solid. The truck travels from the farm to the fields at a bumpy 50 kilometres per hour. The occupants of the truck lie in the bed alongside their tools. They grip the side panels and each other for fear of being thrown overboard. The truck lurches and skids, but maintains a hazardous speed. It reaches the potato pits in eight minutes. The last time the zeks travelled to this spot, it took four hours.

The zeks are ordered out of the truck. They run to the

pits, carrying their creels, picks and shovels. The guard encourages them by striking them lightly with his stick – a warning that a heavier blow could fall at any time. The zeks ascend the ridge. Immediately, they slip on the icy slope and lose their footing. All, without exception, fall over and slide back down. The guard strikes them severely and shouts, "Use your picks, you stupid zeks!" This time, the zeks use the picks to secure a foothold and reach the pits. Sergei's back is stinging from the blows. He is not prepared for the breeze that blows up from the river. Whereas he expected to work in temperatures of -15°, a biting wind blows across the flat landscape and up the river embankment to create a windchill. It feels like -22°. His cheeks smart; his glasses fog over and freeze. He has little time to adjust to the cruel conditions. Another whack on his back directs him to the work at hand. The guard scolds the zeks. "Drive the picks into the ground, you lazy zeks! Break open the pits!" Sergei swings his pick. It strikes the surface, but it does not penetrate the frozen exterior of the pit. He experiences a painful shudder in his arms and along his back. "Strike hard! Put your back into it!" Sergei swings again before the guard inflicts another blow. He swings with all his might. He shuts his eyes and braces for another shock. This time, the pick bites the surface and pierces the shell of the pit. No shudder, this time. He prises the hole and dislodges a chunk of frozen thatch. Once through the surface, the roof of the pit is easily broken and dislodged. The pit is dry and frost-free inside. The potatoes are swiftly gathered into creels. The creels are towed like sleds to the truck and the potatoes are loaded inside. Vladimir stands at the truck with a tin of axle grease in his hand. He daubs grease on the cheeks of each zek saying, "For frostbite. No exposed skin." The zeks find their rhythm. They execute their tasks more skillfully as they repeat the process. The truck is quickly loaded. Vladimir attends to the load in the truck. He ensures that the potatoes are insulated from the cold. When fully loaded, he pulls the cord and the protective cover slides into place. Thereupon, he promptly transports the load to the farm. Meantime, the zeks attack the surface of the next pit.

At the farm, the truck arrives with a full load every 30 minutes – 20 minutes for the round trip plus 5 minutes at each end for loading and unloading. Throughout the morning, they steadily fill the first transport lorry. They attach the trailer which they also fill. At 11:30 am, the lorry departs with the first delivery to the railway siding – one-and-a-half lorryloads equalling a quarter of a railcar. Driving conditions are good. Boris is confident that he will reach the railcars by the nine o'clock deadline.

Back at the farm, Vladimir rotates the farmworkers'

duties. He sends Pyotr to the fields with the truck at noon. This time, the truck brings a container of two-day-old hot cabbage soup to the workers in the pits. Pyotr has the container jammed into the passenger seat of the cab to prevent it from tipping over in transit. At the worksite, the guard grants a 20-minute break. Pyotr hands a steaming mug of soup to each zek. He includes the guard, who is forced to endure the same conditions as the zeks. Sergei is unable to grip the mug in his frigid hands. He places his hands together and cradles the mug like an egg in a cup. After consuming the soup, the zeks are directed to clean their mugs in the river. To accomplish this, they first break the ice at the river's edge and rinse the mugs in the water. Pyotr collects the mugs and places them next to the empty container in the cab. Sergei and several zeks crawl into the bed of the truck and enjoy shelter from the biting wind. Sergei lies on his back, resting on a pile of straw. He looks longingly at the canvas cover stretched above his head – the cover that Pyotr had fastened to prevent the straw from blowing away while the truck was in motion. He reaches his hand up to touch it. If only he could wrap himself in the dry insulating fabric for a few moments, he might restore feeling to his frozen body. His fingers and toes are numb, and his back smarts from the blows to his back. He wonders if he can survive until the end of the workday. And then what? Another day? And if the next day is colder? All too soon, the break is over and the punishing work resumes. At the end of the ten-hour day, 18 truckloads of potatoes had been transported from the pits to the farm. The last truck transports the zeks and the guard back to the prison camp.

The second stage of the delivery – from the farm to the railcars – is progressing well. The first lorry departed before noon. The second lorry is fully loaded, ready to depart first thing on the following morning. And since the potatoes are arriving at the farm faster than the lorries can transport them, six truckloads are stored in the upper level of the storage barn.

At the end of the day, the administrator summons the guards to be present for the daily report. The farm manager attends as a matter of course. Denis addresses the men. "Today, I went to the kitchen to obtain food. The fire was out; the range was cold. It is important to keep the fire burning for a supply of hot water. The only food I could find was a pot of cold cabbage soup. We have plenty of potatoes. The storeroom contains dried fish. Tomorrow, one guard is responsible for the kitchen. And that includes the water cart and the latrines. The second guard will supervise the zeks. There are only ten zeks. This is not a demanding task for one guard. Any question?"

A guard responds. "Which one of us is to do household duties and which one is to guard the zeks?"

"Alternate. Start by flipping a coin. Now go and work it out. Dismissed!"

The guards depart from the office. Denis turns his attention to Vladimir. "Good news to report, I trust?"

"Good news? Yes. But with a caution."

Denis frowns. "Explain what you mean."

Vladimir shifts in his chair and leans forward. "Comrade Lieutenant, you are undoubtedly an excellent prison administrator. But when it comes to farm management some things need to be executed differently. I am concerned about the delivery schedule."

"What's wrong with the delivery schedule? Are you referring to bringing in the crop from the fields, or bringing loaded lorries to the railcars?"

"Both. As it stands, there is no schedule. A structured schedule, with required quotas, will increase efficiency. I am also concerned with the delivery times to the railway siding. We cannot predict the road conditions for any given day. The route is susceptible to blowing snow and icy road conditions." Vladimir leans back in his chair and chooses his words. He prepares to make a statement. "Comrade Administrator, the farm truck takes ten minutes to make the trip from the farm to the pits."

"And back again, I presume."

"Allowing for loading and unloading, each trip, with a full truckload of potatoes, is executed in half an hour. Today we succeeded in bringing 18 truckloads to the farm."

"That's good, is it not?"

"It could be better. Now consider this. Set a daily quota at 24 truckloads; start the workday an hour earlier and conclude only when the quota is reached."

"That would mean working in the dark for part of the day."

"The truck has headlights; the prison has oil lamps. The pits are small confined areas, easily illuminated. And really how much light is needed to gather up potatoes? Keep in mind, we have some degree of daylight, if you consider astronomical twilight, from 6:30 am to 6:15 pm, even though actual daylight occurs between 9:00 am and 4:00 pm."

"Do you think it is possible to bring in 24 truckloads per day? That would mean a 12-hour day."

"I don't believe so. If the daily quota is presented as a challenge, there is a reward at the end of the day – the zeks finish work early if they reach their daily quota." Vladimir leans forward to press his point. "If we can shave three minutes off every loading and unloading, which I believe is feasible, that's six minutes off every round trip. And in the course of a day…"

"That's 120 minutes in a 10-hour day."

"Yes! 24 truckloads in a ten-hour day. Actually, in nine-and-a-half hours. But there is a break for food, of course. At my calculations, the zeks will complete their tasks within 10 hours."

"And if they fail?"

"They work in the dark. Regardless, we get 24 truckloads whether it takes nine-and-a-half hours or ten-and-a-half. And 24 loads per day for five days results in five railcar loads. We gathered 18 truckloads today, so that's a further four-and-a-quarter days to meet target."

"But why fix on 24 loads per day? We are not able to transport that amount to the railcars daily."

"Correct. And that brings me to the next item. Lorry transportation. I have a 5-stage process to ensure efficient delivery to the railcars."

"Spare me the details. You are the expert in managing the delivery details. Give me the one-line summary."

"In a nutshell, the transport lorries operate 24 hours a day; drivers alternate; there is a period allowed for refuelling and service. Two deliveries per day equalling three loads – thanks to the trailers. One railcar is filled every two days. All five will be filled in ten days. No, in 11 days. There should be a day of rest in there to prevent worker burnout."

"So, the railcars should be ready to roll on day 12. That would be 27 December."

"Correct! Or the ministry may keep to their schedule and move the railcars on 31 December."

"That's good news. But you have not answered my question. Why is it important to move 24 loads of potatoes daily from the pits? That's double the rate at which we transport the crop to the railway. And the surplus potatoes require storage."

"That is correct. Potatoes come in from the fields at a rate equal to 6 lorryloads per day. The transport lorries are fitted with trailers so, for them, two trips daily to the railway equals 3 lorryloads." Vladimir hesitates for dramatic effect. Then says in a whisper, "But what happens if you lose the zek labour?"

Denis Novak thinks back to the commitment made by the inspector. 'The 10 zeks are yours until the end of December, or until they are needed at another labour camp.' He considers the significance of the inspector's statement. Zeks are highly mobile. Other labour camps require zek labour. Priorities unexpectedly shift. The administrator remembers another comment, 'Don't forget, the permanent farm staff remains with the farm.' Denis has little faith in the 'clowns in Moscow' who lack an understanding of how a labour farm operates. He responds to Vladimir. "If the zeks are removed and we rely solely on the farm staff, how long will it take to fill the railcars?"

"I estimate 22 days."

"That's well into January. And well past the deadline."

"If we keep the zeks for another five days, and they produce at the rate I propose, we should meet the deadline."

"I see. So, we push them like hell for the next five days.

And hope that we retain the labour force throughout this period. You are smart, Comrade Kotyakov, to set a daily quota for the field workers – 24 truckloads per day. I'll instruct the guards to energize the zeks to meet this objective. You, Comrade, will see to your end of things."

*   *   *   *   *

The zeks' experience is quite different at the end of that harsh day. There is no service in the dining hall. The guard from the fields ushers them into the kitchen and directs them to get the fire going. He obtains a pot of potato soup from the larder and some stale bread. The zeks are left to fend for themselves. The guard joins them. When the soup is hot, one of the zeks acts as the cook and ladles soup into bowls. He manages to pour more than the prescribed single ladle-full measure into each bowl. The guard seems unaware, or perhaps, does not care. He accepts the same ration of food. At the end of the meal, he instructs them to clean up the kitchen and retire to the dormitory. Thereupon, he leaves them unattended and unsupervised. One brave zek sneaks to the front door. It is locked. They conclude that they are securely locked inside the building, but have limited freedom of movement inside. So, with nothing else to do, the fatigued zeks go to bed. Sergei, along with most of the other zeks, feels the lingering stings from the day's bruises. His hands and feet have recovered from numbness. But they sting painfully. The dormitory is cold, close to freezing, and offers sparse comfort. He is unable to sleep because of the pain. After a sleepless hour, he decides to walk to alleviate the aches. Outside, in the corridor, he encounters the guard. The guard questions him. Sergei informs him of his discomfort. The guard acknowledges that it is cold. Furthermore, he is on his way to the kitchen to obtain warmth. He invites Sergei to join him. The guard who struck him at work is offering comfort. It is a paradox, of course, and just one of the many absurdities of life in a labour camp. In the kitchen, they both consume hot potato tea. Back at the dormitory, the guard orders Sergei to wait in the corridor. The guard enters the staff dormitory and returns moments later with an extra blanket for Sergei.

Sergei feels compelled to say something. "Thank you, Comrade Guard. Shall I see you again tomorrow?"

"No. Yury is your guard tomorrow. I am on housekeeping duties. And just to forewarn you, you start an hour earlier tomorrow, and a daily quota is set. You'll be forced to improve on today's performance."

Sergei looks to the next day with trepidation. He already feels the stinging blows he expects to receive at work.

CHAPTER TWELVE

FINAL LOAD FOR MOSCOW

On 15 December, the zeks are roundly awakened at 6:30 am. It is still dark. Sergei attempts to rise from his bed. His muscles are stiff from the previous day's work. It agonizes him to move. The sight of an approaching guard gives him the required motivation to ignore his pain. He rises before a stick strikes him. They have 20 minutes to dress, obtain a ladle of potato soup and don their winter work clothes. They arrive at the pits, in the astronomical twilight, a little before 7:00 am. Sergei experiences pain with every movement. He has difficulty getting out of the truck and walking to the potato pit. He considers stepping out of line to invite a response from the guard. Slow work invites a beating; breaking out of line results in his being shot. Sergei considers the pain of death. It has to be less painful than the gruelling work he must undergo. He foregoes the notion, at least for the moment. His aches might ease as the work progresses.

When the truck brings food at 11:00 am. Mikhail, the driver, opens the passenger-side door and invites the zeks to partake of cabbage soup. The guard grants a 20-minute break. Many of the zeks take advantage of the break to relieve their bladders. They descend the embankment to the riverside. Thereafter, they join the other zeks in the queue for a ladle of soup. Sergei is with neither group. He had hoped that the rhythm of the work would produce some relief to his aching body. This is not the case. If anything, his suffering has increased. His muscles ache; his feet and hands are numb from the cold: he has experienced another beating. He breaks from the group and walks to the back of the truck. At first, it appears that he is joining the queue. Instead, he lowers the tailgate and crawls onto the bed of the truck. He slides towards the mound of straw, and like the previous day, he lies on his back and stares up at the canvas cover. The guard's attention is on the group at the river. He gestures to them to join the queue. Then, he too approaches the soup container and obtains his portion of soup. Sergei lies in wait for the guard to find him and shoot him. Minutes pass. The guard has not yet noticed that a zek is missing. Sergei considers the comfort of the dry insulating cover above his head. The cover is only a metre-and-a-half above the floor of the truck bed. Sergei has no trouble squeezing under the cover and over the roller. It is painful, but not troublesome. He slides over the roller and into the pocket of the canvas. He is suspended from the roller as in a cocoon. The canvas is as comfortable as a hammock, albeit somewhat rough. Thus insulated from the cold, Sergei's body recovers its warmth. He relaxes and resigns himself to his fate.

The guard blows his whistle to signal a return to work. The zeks line up. It is only at this point that he realizes that he is one zek short. The guard is confused. Should he go and search for the missing zek? After all, the missing zek is probably down by the river where some of the zeks go during their break. He mounts the ridge and scans the riverbank. There is no sign of the missing zek. He remembers that some zeks lie in the bed of the truck during their break, so he examines the truck. The sagging canvas supported by the roller appears normal. He checks inside the truck, under the truck and all around the truck. He concludes that one zek has truly disappeared. Because there is only one guard, he cannot leave the nine zeks unattended while he attempts to locate the missing one. His only option is to have Mikhail return to the farm in the empty truck and sound the alarm. As Mikhail drives off, the guard makes the nine zeks stand in line. He brandishes his handgun, lest another zek is emboldened to flee. Any zek who breaks the line will be shot.

On the journey back to the farm, Mikhail is unaware of the uninvited passenger hidden within the rolled-up cover. He mutters to himself. "A zek has gone off. That's a prison problem; not a farm problem. But now I, and the other farmworkers, will be dragged into a manhunt. As if I don't have enough to do as it is. Drive to the pits today, drive to the railway tomorrow. I'm lucky if I'll get five hours of sleep tonight. And now **this**?"

The bumpy ride alerts Sergei. He had been in the comfort zone between sleep and coziness – awake but not fully cognizant. At first, he is disappointed that the guard had not shot him. He laughs at his irrationality. He realizes that he has escaped the guard. He wonders how far this subterfuge will take him. His brain clicks into gear. He calls upon his ingenuity and resourcefulness to find a way to flee from the labour camp. But he needs time to devise a plan. For the moment, he remains still. His adrenalin is rushing. His pain no longer troubles him.

Mikhail reaches the perimeter of the farm. He drives along the security fence to the access road to enter through the gate. He stops within sight of the gate. As expected, the gate is unmanned – a shortage of guards. He reckons that this might be his only chance to relive his bladder and light a cigarette, at least for some time. He exits the truck and proceeds to the side of the road. No sooner has he done this, than Boris drives up. Boris is returning from the railway with a shipment of dried fish and cabbage and the post. He draws up alongside the farm truck and shouts, "Mikhail! What are you doing stopped at the side of the road? And are you coming back from the fields with no load?"

Mikhail waves at Boris. "Ah, one of the zeks has gone missing and I'm on my way to alert the camp. I'm taking a break for a quick piss while I have the chance."

"One of the zeks is missing? Well, that will put the fox among the hens. But listen, let me enter ahead of you and park the lorry inside the service garage. I want to be gone before you sound the alarm."

Sergei listens to the chat. He grabs this unexpected opportunity to creep out of the farm truck and into the transportation lorry. Boris drives into the farmyard through the unmanned gateway by activating the To/Fro Balanced Hinge. He comes to a stop inside the service garage. Upon observing this, Mikhail enters the yard and sounds his horn with the recognized alarm signal – a series of three triple-blasts. Four men come running to him – the administrator, the farm manager, Pyotr and Gregori.

The administrator shouts, "What's the alarm?"

"A zek has gone missing from the work field! He was there at the break – at eleven. He was gone when they lined up to resume work."

Lieutenant Denis Novak is an experienced soldier. He

knows all the tricks. He shouts to the two farmworkers, "The truck. Search the truck. Every inch. Unfurl the cover. Do not leave a centimetre unchecked!" The search takes a few seconds. It reveals nothing untoward. Meanwhile, Vladimir runs to the service garage and fetches his binoculars. Denis continues to give instructions. "Everyone on the truck! Two men on the outside bumper over the engine. Two more hanging on the running boards – one on each side." He rides the front bumper with Vladimir. "Keep your eyes peeled for footprints in the snow. If the zek is canny, he will know to walk in the tire tracks. But he must leave the path at some point. Otherwise, we'll drive into him. He could not have reached this point yet; no zek is fit enough to go five kilometres in half an hour."

They reach the pits in six minutes. The administrator is satisfied that the missing zek did not go in the direction of the farm. He questions the guard, who swears that he was vigilant at all times. The guard is certain that none of the zeks left the area. Yet, one is missing. They survey the work area. It is a small area. The surrounding snow is undisturbed. The only footprints leading away from the pits are to the river. Denis inspects the river. He sees where the ice has been broken to access the water. The ice is close to the river's edge. Farther out, it is too thin to support the weight of a man. The centre current flows swiftly and is completely ice-free.

Vladimir views the distant riverbank through his binoculars. He informs the administrator. "No footprints on the far bank. If the zek attempted to cross the river, he perished – either by drowning or from hypothermia."

Both men stand in silence for a moment. They wonder if the zek deliberately took his own life. Denis shouts to the guard. "Which zek was it? The one missing?"

He shouts back, "Sergei Falkov."

Denis mutters, "The inventor."

And Vladimir adds, "The innovator."

The two men consider the possibility that the genius zek may have outfoxed them. They question the guard in depth. And they question the zeks with the threat of punishment. Afterwards, they repeat the search process. Two hours later, they conclude that Sergei Falkov is missing and presumed dead. Most likely a mishap from drowning while accessing water through broken ice.

The guard, with his gun in hand, is still watching the nine zeks standing in line. The administrator instructs them to recommence work. The zeks take to their work eagerly. They are frozen from standing in the cold. The physical exertion will get their blood circulating. Secondly, the activity reduces the risk of the guard shooting any of them. The guard holsters his handgun. The zeks concentrate on the work. The potatoes start to pile into the truck bed. Three minutes later, the truck departs with a load of potatoes. Lieutenant Novak, Vladimir and the two farmworkers ride the running boards back to the farm.

The daily quota falls short. Only 17 truckloads of potatoes reach the farm.

Later that evening, at the daily meeting, Denis and Vladimir discuss the events of the day. Vladimir reassures the administrator. "The misfortune of losing a zek does not alter the rate at which we load the railcars. That is still on schedule."

Denis nods. "True. But it raises some concerns. If I report the death of a zek…"

"The ministry has no regard for a zek's life. Why worry about that?"

The administrator raises a finger and continues. "If I report the death of a zek, the ministry may look at our labour requirements. They will see from my reports that the railcars are being loaded on time. They may conclude that we don't need any zeks at all."

"So, what are you saying?"

"I will delay advising them of the death of a zek until later."

"Until we no longer require the zek labour. Good. And on the matter of zek labour, the plan needs to be revised."

"Revised?"

"Yes. Due to the reduced labour force, my proposed schedule of moving 24 truckloads of potatoes from the pits is altered to 21 loads per day. We also lost two hours of work today."

"It was 18 loads yesterday; 17 today. And you say that it ought to be 21 per day from tomorrow?"

"Yes. And in five days the full complement will be filled."

"That's two days longer than your first estimate, December 20. That's when I will report the death of the zek. Or better still. I will wait until the cargo is fully loaded on railcars and ready for shipment to Moscow."

"Just so long as you wait until **all** the potatoes are stored."

"**All** the potatoes? There are more?"

"Judging from the contents of the pits, I believe that the yield will be greater than the quota."

"A surplus? By how much?"

I don't know yet. But significantly more than the required quota of five loaded railcars. I propose that we drive the zeks to maintain their daily quota until the entire crop is stored – however long it takes."

Denis Novak has another reason to delay reporting the loss of a zek. He will require zek labour for a while longer than originally estimated. And then there is the question of the surplus. If it is substantial, it raises a problem. He wonders if he is required to report a surplus yield after the quota is reached and delivered. He smiles. How could a surplus be a problem?

The following day, 16 December, goes according to plan. Two transport lorries, with trailers, depart at 8:00 am. They return after midnight, between one and two o'clock, whereupon they are loaded again by the outgoing drivers assisted by the fresh alternate drivers. When loaded, they park the lorries inside the service garage for a maintenance check before departing once more at 8:00 am, driven, this time, by the alternate drivers. Throughout the day, the zeks manage to load 21 truckloads of potatoes. At the storage barn, two farmworkers, utilizing crates and winches, haul the crop to the upper level. Later, they will use chutes to rapidly fill the transport lorries.

On 23 December, the last truckload of potatoes is extracted from the pits. When tallied, the store of potatoes exceeds the quota by 25 truckloads – more than the equivalent of two railcars. On 24 December, the zeks perform routine light duties as they did in November. Transportation to the railway goes according to plan. The final load is scheduled for 26 December. Once loaded onto the railcars and the waybill is lodged with the stationmaster, the consignment becomes the responsibility of the railway company. The cargo of potatoes could be dispatched as early as 27 December, four days ahead of the deadline. Corrective Farm No.47 will have fulfilled its quota and its obligation.

On 24 December, the administrator instructs the farm manager to draw up the bill of lading. It will be delivered to the stationmaster with the final lorryload. Lieutenant Denis Novak will be relieved when the stationmaster accepts it. It will mark the successful conclusion to the harvest – mission accomplished. There is one other matter to attend to. The labour camp's prison facility will be vacated until the next labour requirement. He drafts his concluding report to the ministry. It addresses the reassignment of the two remaining guards and the nine zeks. He lists the names of the guards and zeks. He refers to the loss of one zek that occurred during the winter harvesting, one named Sergei Falkov. Denis is satisfied that this should complete his final report. He reads through it to check for errors. He hesitates at the name 'Sergei Falkov'. "Sergei Falkov," he murmurs aloud, "is the only zek I ever encountered that was rehabilitated. His loss is our loss. Had he lived and endured the harsh labour, he could have been of service to the state long before the completion of his sentence." He sighs. Satisfied with the report, he signs it and places it in a sealed addressed envelope. This report will be delivered to the post with the final load to the railway. He deliberately omitted a reference to the surplus potatoes in storage. First, the ministry did not ask for an updated harvest report. Fulfillment of the quota is the only requirement. Secondly, collective farms are permitted to retain surplus crops for their own consumption once their quota is rendered. The inference, in this situation, is that the surplus belongs to the farm – a distinction between the labour camp and the farm operation.

Vladimir is entrusted to drive the final lorry to the railway and lodge the waybill documents for a cargo of five fully-loaded railcars of potatoes. He is further directed to post the administrator's final report and send a telegram to the ministry advising them of the delivery status.

Denis Novak sleeps well on the night of 25 December.

On 26 December, Vladimir delivers the final lorryload of potatoes. On 27 December, sometime after midnight, he arrives back at the labour camp. At daybreak, he enters the administrator's office to deliver the post he had picked up at the railway station. He reports that the consignment was properly executed and that he sent a telegram to advise the ministry. In their reply, they acknowledged that the waybill was communicated to them by the railway company. Denis nods at hearing this. It is what he expected. He is relieved that the episode of 'potatoes for Moscow' is finally closed. After a few tense months at Corrective Farm No.47, he is optimistic that, in the end, his performance will be recognized and acknowledged favourably. He accepts the post handed to him by Vladimir. There is one sole envelope marked 'PRIORITY' and bears the stamp 'MINISTRY OF THE INTERIOR'. Denis eagerly opens the envelope. He removes a cluster of pages and glances at the top sheet. His jaw drops.

CHAPTER THIRTEEN

THE SERVICE GARAGE

During the frenzy in the labour camp upon learning of the missing zek, Sergei remains motionless in his new hiding spot in the transportation lorry. Just before the alarm is sounded, Boris drives the lorry into the farmyard through the unmanned gateway by activating the To/Fro Balanced Hinge. He comes to a stop inside the service garage. He turns off the engine and sits quietly. He hears Mikhail sound the alarm by honking the truck's horn. Thereupon, the clatter of running feet and the din of excited voices resonate from the yard. Vladimir comes bursting into the garage and enters his office. Within seconds, he reappears carrying a pair of binoculars. He runs back to the centre of the hubbub. Moments later, Boris hears the sound of the departing truck. The administrator's cries fade into the distance. He extricates himself from the driver's seat. He speaks loudly, addressing no one in particular in the spacious garage. "On the road for 24 hours – not counting the two-hour break at the taverna on the Volga Highway in Naberezhnye Morkvashi. On the road for 24 hours – and not counting the stop to pick up the food supplies to replenish the store. On the road for 24 hours. My shift is done. I'm done." Boris hauls the goods from his lorry – a box of dried fish and three sacks of cabbage. He carries the box, and drags the bags, to the food store, shutting the garage door as he exits.

Sergei is at the peak of alertness. When the lorry enters the garage and before it comes to a complete stop, he pokes his head through the concealment of the straw and takes stock of his surroundings. Ignoring his pain, he slips stealthily from the lorry and hides behind a stack of planks. He waits until all is quiet. Vladimir enters and leaves. Boris departs. Five minutes later, he ventures out from behind the stack of timber. Satisfied that he is alone, he surveys the enormous garage for a secure refuge. Being familiar with the service garage, he chooses a loft location where tires are stored. There are many nooks and crannies in the loft. Should anyone enter, he will hear him mount the ladder in sufficient time to sneak further into the dark corners. Should someone require a set of tires, those closest to the ladder will be chosen. Years could pass before anyone ventures to the dimly-lit distant recesses. He arranges some tires to form a comfortable seat. Then he lies down and figures out a plan.

Sergei is familiar with the work schedules in the garage. When men enter, he listens and identifies the tasks being performed. He recognizes who is present and who is working. And the lights from the lamps betray the whereabouts of the men as they move about. He discovers, through Vladimir's instructions, that the lorries are to be loaded and parked in the garage overnight. He also learns the revised routines regarding driver rotation and delivery schedules. This is valuable information.

At 9:00 pm, work ceases in the garage. The men leave. Sergei feels his way from the loft and down to the familiar floor of the garage. The farm truck and both lorries are parked inside. He locates a lamp in its accustomed spot by the door. He lights it from the flame in the stove. His priority is to check the integrity of the window covers. The covers are intended to prevent frost from entering the garage through the windows. They also block the light. Sergei is satisfied that the light from his lamp is undetectable from outside the building. He examines the vehicles. He establishes that the transport lorries, with trailers attached, are filled with potatoes and are thoroughly insulated and securely covered. This is in keeping with the new delivery schedule. Next, he places the lamp at the stove. He checks the door of the garage. He opens it a fraction. He is surprised that it is not locked, notwithstanding that a lock is installed. The door makes a scraping noise when opening. He shuts it. Had anyone glimpsed the light through the fractionally-opened door, it would appear to be from the flickering stove. Sergei berates himself for having opened the door. It could have raised someone's curiosity about how the light from the stove appeared and disappeared. Next time, if there is a next time, he will need to block the light. Easy to do. Turn off the lamp and shut the stove door.

Minutes later, he is satisfied that his presence has gone undetected. He invigorates the fire in the stove from the stack of wood. There are dregs of potato tea in the saucepan. He heats it and consumes the warm beverage. He also locates a heel of left-over bread. He eats it. Sergei experiences relief from the food and the warmth of the stove. But it is no time to rest. He is strengthened and emboldened. He obtains tools from the carpenter's workbench. Then he checks the door to the manager's office. It is locked as expected. He unscrews the hinges on the door and opens it. Next, he cuts and files the lock bolt to within a few centimetres of flush. He checks his measurements and when satisfied, he replaces the door and secures the hinges. Now to test his work. Using a length of wood, he leans against the door jamb and pushes against the opposite side. There is a little give in the wooden jambs and they bow a fraction. The resulting space is sufficient to pop open the door. He manages to shut the door by repeating the same procedure. Sergei has executed the first stage of his plan – he has access to the manager's office at any time with relative ease. The manager will continue to lock and unlock the door and be none the wiser about the modification. The crafty innovator cleans the area and removes all traces of his work. He replaces the tools.

Sergei is not finished with executing his plan. He enters the manager's office and chooses specific keys from the hooks. Then he extinguishes the lamp and squeezes out through the garage door. He makes sure to nudge it a fraction at a time to minimize the noise. He treads quietly through the deserted yard. His first stop is the food store. He chooses the appropriate key and enters. This door is silent. He feels his way around, guided by his nose. He obtains a piece of dried fish and a whole cabbage. He exits. Next, he makes his way to the supply store. He passes the huts where the farmworkers sleep. All is quiet. He continues stealthily. In the supply store, he locates soap. By slapping the shelves, he identifies where the clothing is stored. He recognizes trousers and tunics. Working his way farther along the shelves, he encounters a greatcoat. He puts it on. He continues like this until he acquires shirts, socks and underwear. He loads up with as much as he can carry.

Back in the service garage, he relights the lamp. He is pleased with the clothing. It is army-issue clothing for the farmworkers. He has acquired shirts, socks, and underwear. He also has trousers and a tunic. Later, maybe on another night, he will attempt to find boots and a hat. His next priority is to wash himself. He is aware that he smells like a zek. When the men arrive in the garage, he might be located by anyone tracing the odour. He pours some drinking water from the bucket into a pot and heats it. He pours the hot water into a metal container to serve as a basin. Using a rag, he washes thoroughly. He dresses in his new clothes. He rips his zek clothing into shreds and burns them in the firepit of the stove. From the carpenter's workbench, he selects a cutting blade. Then, he shaves his face with the aid of the lorry's mirror. When he is finished, he examines his face. He does not recognize himself. His wild beard is gone, and there is no trace of his once-elegant goatee. This is the first time Sergei has been clean-shaven since he first went to college. He studies the unfamiliar face in the mirror. He moves the lamp to different angles; he puckers his mouth and tilts his head; he even pinches his cheeks. He is amazed that this is his face. It is the face of a stranger. He considers cutting his unkempt hair. Since he is mostly bald, he decides to shave off what remains. He speaks to his reflection. "Sergei, from this moment on, you are a new man." Next, he tears strips off his newly acquired cabbage and places them in the pot on the stove. He cuts a few strips off the dried fish and tosses them in. He adds water and heats his stew-soup concoction. When the contents are cooked, he gets his favourite bent mug from the hook and fills it from the pot. He refills it over again until he consumes the entire amount.

Sergei is getting anxious about the time. The clock in the manager's office indicates that it is 4:55 am. It is time to clear up all traces of his presence. First, he checks the office. The keys are back on the appropriate hooks. He exits and 'locks' the door. He rinses the saucepan, pot and mug into his 'basin', which he empties, in turn, in the latrine. He gathers his hair clippings and casts them onto the fire. He searches for an alternative lamp. He finds one on a shelf. It is dusty and empty. It is a lamp that is not used frequently. He fills it from the paraffin can – a procedure he has frequently observed. He lights his 'new' lamp and extinguishes the other, which he places back in its designated spot. Lastly, he gathers up his soap and rag, his stock of new-found clothing and his supply of food. He proceeds to his pad in the loft. He hides his things next to his 'bed'. With a sense of satisfaction, he lies on the greatcoat on a mattress of tires and extinguishes his lamp. Until he executes the next stage of his plan, this loft location is his flat, adequately provisioned for comfortable living.

The next day, Sergei listens to the men work and talk together. There is no mention of anything missing from the food store or the supply store. Vladimir and Pyotr arrive at 7:00 am. Pyotr is assigned to drive the farm truck. He departs before 8:00 am to take the zeks to the pits. The assigned lorry drivers are Gregori and Mikail. They arrive at 8:00 am and depart for the railway station. Vladimir and Boris remain at the farm to load potatoes in the storage barn whenever the truck returns from the pits. Vladimir criticizes Boris for the clumsy way in which he stored the fish and cabbage upon his return to the farm. The guard on housekeeping duties had complained to Vladimir that the fish box was partly open, and one of the cabbage bags was ripped at the top. He noticed it when he fetched cabbages for the zeks' morning soup. Boris apologizes and figures it must have been due to the rough way he dropped the fish box onto the shelf and the jerky manner in which he dragged the bags across the yard. He pleads that he was tired after driving for 24 hours. Vladimir orders him to place a pot on the stove and boil potatoes.

That night, Sergei repeats his foray into the supply store. This time, he allows more time for an exhaustive examination of the contents. He discovers the supply of boots. He takes his time to select a pair that fits his comfort. He is unable to determine their appearance, but if they fit, they are right for him. He hunts for a winter hat. He finds a fur hat with a metal button on the front – the customary Soviet emblem, he assumes. And stored on the shelf beside the hats are gloves: not bulky mitts, but well-fitting gloves. Back in the garage, he adds these items to his stock of clothing. Next, he cooks and consumes a meal. After removing all evidence of his presence, he retires to his lair in the loft. He laughs to himself. He considers himself to be the most comfortable zek in all of Russia. However, he reminds himself that he is still a zek and, if he is discovered, he is a dead zek.

Another day passes. On the following night, Sergei waits until the loaded lorries are parked in the garage. It is past 2:00 am. He has three hours to spend preparing the next stage of his plan. He foregoes food. He enters the manager's office. He rummages through the collection of papers and forms in the office. He studies the many stamps on inkpads. He examines them by reading the inverted lettering and symbols. His plan progresses. He inserts pages into the typewriter and begins to type – waybills, consignment forms, acknowledgments, confirmations, reference letters and letters of instruction. When finished typing, he reads the results of his work. Satisfied with his collection of papers, he selects a stamp, wets it on the ink pad, and thumps it on the top sheet. He startles himself by the sound. It echoes throughout the spacious garage. He worries that it may have sounded through the walls and was audible from the outside. He applies more stamps, this time by silently rolling them until all the pages are plastered in stamps – stamps of approval, stamps of authorization, stamps confirming the stamps. He examines his handiwork and jokes aloud. "Russia loves papers covered in stamps. The stamps bear a stronger message than the text. I wonder if many people just react to the stamps and decline to read the written message. Bureaucracy." Lastly, he applies illegible signatures with scrolling flourishes. That's another thing bureaucrats love – flowery signatures. He assembles his papers, clears the desk and leaves the office as he found it – except for the undetectable missing papers. His plan is progressing but is without a realistic resolution. If he fails, he is caught and shot. If he succeeds, he is caught and shot – eventually. Travelling through Stalin's Russia requires 'papers'. Papers are checked at intervals and at frequent checkpoints. Travelling by passenger train is a non-starter. He is unable to obtain a ticket, let alone pass a transit inspection. Unless he is a potato. The potatoes are bound for export. At some point, the railcars containing the cargo from Corrective Farm No.47 must reach an exit port or a border crossing. If he is to travel like a potato, he needs to travel by goods train with 'export papers'. It is 5:30 am. He retires to his secret lair for the third night. Alone in the quiet of the loft, he consumes raw cabbage and cold fish.

On night number four, he enters the manager's office. This time he rummages through past files. Eventually, he finds what he is looking for – copies of export forms. These forms contain the heading 'Ministry of Industry and Trade'. They appear to be 'received-in-good-order' acknowledgements of goods for export. They also state the intended 'End Countries'. In every case, Germany is listed as the ultimate destination. Sergei nods his head in understanding. Ever since the Treaty of Rapallo in 1922, Russia and Germany have enjoyed friendly trade relations, much to the condemnation of France and Britain. And Russia's top exports are wheat and potatoes. Sergei exclaims, "Just as I thought, the potatoes are going to Germany!" He considers the routing process. The cargo from the farm is delivered to the Ministry of Agriculture in Moscow, transferred to the Ministry of Industry and Trade, which combines it with cargos from other farms. In due course, the ministry completes bills of lading and export permits for an entire train – as many as 50 railcars bound for Germany. Sergei has found the missing link in his plan.

The inventor/innovator studies the export forms. Like all Russian government documents, they bear multiple stamps. Sergei digs through the pile of paper until he finds an export form with an almost-blank final page, one similarly covered in official stamps. He removes the sheet and goes to the typewriter. He writes confusing and complex information on the page. He makes heightened references to 'Potato Export'. He phrases his words to emulate the officialese of the authentic document. When finished, it looks very official, even if it makes little sense. The new lettering matches the original line. All government typewriters have the same type. A close inspection would reveal a minor difference, mostly in the fresher ink of Sergei's composition. The greatest risk is in someone cross-checking the referenced file at the ministry.

On this night, like the other nights, he covers his tracks and retreats to the solitude of his den. He counsels himself to caution. He must move at an opportune time. It's not tonight. Sergei bides his time for the present. He remains in the garage, a hidden boarder in the loft.

CHAPTER FOURTEEN

GOODS TO MOSCOW

Over the succeeding days, Sergei attempts to ascertain what is occurring in the camp and what outside events are relevant. Daily, he listens to the men talking in the garage. At night, he studies whatever material is on the manager's desk. He learns that he is presumed dead. Hence, there is no active search for the missing zek. That's good to know. The entire crop of potatoes has been brought to storage on the farm. As a result, the farmworkers are likely to spend more working time in the garage. That's also good to know. He increases his vigilance in concealing his presence. The most important information he learns is the delivery date of the final load to the railway – scheduled for 26 December. Sergei, to his distress, realizes that he does not know what day it is. Is it due to depart tomorrow, or sometime within the next four days? The only clue is that the final delivery will be by a single lorry and not by two lorries. So that night, and every night, he inspects the loaded lorries in the garage. At some point, there will be only one instead of two. He continues to examine the manager's desk for clues. Vladimir keeps a calendar hanging on the wall. But he does not mark off the days. And he does not keep an appointment diary. Sergei prepares for imminent departure. He selects clean travel clothes suitable for his needs; he shaves every day; he packs food for a journey, which he places in the inside pockets of his greatcoat – black bread and boiled potatoes. He is anxious. He spends most of his time surveying the activity in the garage.

On 25 December, Sergei learns which day it is. Vladimir announces that he will drive the final lorry. He will deliver the waybill and transit documents to the railway company upon arrival. Thereupon, when the railcars are finally loaded to capacity, they will be ready to move. Vladimir will depart with the final load on the following morning at 8:00 am.

It is past midnight when the lorries return from the railway siding, having delivered their loads for the 25th. Boris drives an empty lorry into the garage and parks next to the farm truck. Then, he assists Pyotr and Vladimir in loading the second lorry at the storage barn. It is after 2:00 am when Vladimir drives the loaded lorry into the garage. He enters his office and picks up the required delivery documents. He places them in the cab next to the driver's seat. He executes a quick inspection of the lorry and checks the security of the cover. When satisfied, he extinguishes the light and leaves the garage. The garage falls silent and is cast into darkness, except for the faint flicker of the burning fire in the stove.

Sergei prepares for the next stage of his plan – to embark on his journey to freedom. He cooks one last meal – fish boiled with potatoes. Afterwards, he removes evidence of the meal. He enters the loft and dresses in winter clothing. There are two spacious inner pockets in his greatcoat. He deposits his food in one of them. The second pocket serves as his bank of official-looking documents. Alas, he lacks money and a weapon. Consequently, he must rely on his ingenuity and tenacity to carry through.

The loaded lorry is parked facing the doorway. It is prepared for a prompt exit. The cargo is adequately protected from the winter elements. The cover is taut and securely fastened, due mostly to Sergei's innovative roller mechanism. He releases the fasteners and pulls the cord. The cover rolls back smoothly. Sergei examines the load. It is firmly packed and is layered in insulating straw. He rearranges the straw to form a pocket. He determines that this will effectively accommodate him and conceal him from a visual inspection. He pats the straw to form a trenchlike pathway to crawl through. When he is satisfied with his preparations, he steps out of the cargo bed and secures the cover to its previous state. He extinguishes the lamp. He waits a few minutes to adjust his vision to the darkness. A faint glow emanates from the red embers in the stove. Now for the delicate part. Sergei squeezes under the tarpaulin and crawls along his straw-lined trench. He is careful to avoid disturbing the cover. He feels his way along in the darkness, pushing loose straw behind him as he moves. He reaches the prepared pocket. He settles in and covers himself in straw.

Sometime later, he hears the scraping sound of the garage door being pulled open. He listens to the sound of a man entering the garage – Vladimir, he presumes. Sergei construes what is happening from what he hears. The canvas cover is tugged to check for tautness; the tire pressure is checked, the fuel tank is filled; the starting handle is cranked. The truck engine kicks and starts on the third attempt. As the engine warms, the choke is eased back until the engine throbs smoothly. The gears are engaged and the lorry moves out from the garage. It stops and remains stationary while Vladimir shuts the garage door. Sergei thinks to himself that he omitted to install To/Fro Balanced Hinges on the garage door. They probably wouldn't have worked, anyway, on a door that drags on the ground. Sergei feels the motion of the lorry on the stony surface of the farmyard. The lorry stops twice as Vladimir activates the levers to open and shut the main gate. Thereafter, the crunch of the tires on the frozen gravel of the access road produces a rhythmic lulling sound. If the driving conditions are good, the trip should take nine hours and the lorry should reach the rail siding by 5:00 pm.

After drifting in and out of sleep over countless hours, Sergei finally notices the sound of the lorry shifting to a lower gear. He is jolted by a lurch. He remembers that the access road to the rail siding is rough. The lorry stops moving and remains stationary with the engine idling. It is time to make a move. He crawls to his burrow-like opening and gently lifts the edge of the cover, high enough to peer outside. The lorry has stopped alongside the five railcars. He hears Vladimir exit the cab and, moments later, he sees him walk in the direction of the station. The farm manager steps over a series of railway tracks, making his way from the lorry to the railway office. Four railway workers spot him and approach him. Sergei observes them talking and gesturing towards the lorry. Vladimir waves his documents at them. They point him in the direction of the office. While they are thus engaged, Sergei sneaks from the lorry and walks to the railcars. He is indiscernible to the men on the other side. He must choose a railcar. Which one is the first car and which one is the last? He decides on the middle car as the one least likely to invite attention. He climbs the ladder and enters the space between two cars. The railway workers reach the lorry. One of them drives it closer to the last railcar (or first railcar) to accommodate a convenient transfer of the load. Thereupon, they employ themselves to their task. Unobserved, Sergei climbs to the roof of the railcar, opens one of the hatches and drops inside. The car is fully loaded, but the top layer of straw gives him enough space to shut the hatch and lie low. Sergei realizes that he has no way of determining how long he needs to remain concealed in the railcar. Will it depart later today? Or tomorrow? Or in some days hence? He accepts that this is his new loft accommodation for the next while – only no available stove to cook food. Regardless, he is on his journey. He wonders how long it will take to reach Moscow. A goods train makes frequent stops to hook or unhook railcars as it accepts additional loads or drops off those that reach their destination. The journey could take an entire day.

Early on the following morning, Sergei is rudely awakened by a loud jolt. The railcar is moving, then colliding, jostling to and fro. The railcars are being shunted into order. When the car finally comes to rest, the five potato-laden cars are hooked to an engine on the main tracks. Except that Sergei is oblivious of the exact circumstances of his location. He considers opening a hatch a fraction to peer out. He places his hand against the hatch, but before he pushes it open, the hatch is lifted. Sergei stares in surprise at a pair of eyes staring back down at him in equal surprise. It is the train guard inspecting the integrity of the railcars in a routine check. Sergei reacts quickly and decisively. He had prepared for such an encounter. He extricates the papers from his inner pocket and waves them officiously. "I'm from Corrective Farm No.47. I am to accompany the cargo to its destination."

The guard glances briefly at the papers, as if uninterested, or maybe unimpressed. He exclaims with a degree of annoyance, "Get out of the car! And come with me." He gestures to Sergei to exit the car.

Back on the platform, the guard checks waybills on his clipboard. He addresses the stationmaster who is standing by. "Goods checked. Cars are secure. Clear to depart." The stationmaster nods in acknowledgement and strides to the front of the train. The guard, with Sergei in tow, walks towards the rear of the train. He picks up a postbag from the platform in passing the Post & Telegraph office. He instructs Sergei to enter the guard's van.

At this point, Sergei understands that he is not arrested. The grumpy guard simply wants him to travel in the guard's van at the rear of the train. The guard enters and tosses the postbag on the floor. Then, he leans out the side window and flips a coloured paddle to communicate to the engineer that the checking is complete and the train is ready to depart. The stationmaster passes the baton to the engineer, thereby passing authoritative control to him. The train moves forward.

The guard's van is a busy place. The guard opens the postbag and sorts letters into pigeonholes. At intervals, he empties the contents of a pigeonhole into a postbag. He hangs the selected postbag on a pole attached to a mechanized lever. He activates the lever and the pole swings out from the train at right angles. It interacts with similar poles attached to an elevated platform at the side of the tracks. When the two sets of poles interact, the postbag is deposited outside, and a new bag is snagged and brought into the van. All this occurs while the train is in motion. What Sergei witnesses is a postal exchange. The guard sorts the newly-obtained letters. These exchanges occur frequently along the route. Sometimes, an item is too heavy for the process. In these cases, the train makes a brief stop to accommodate the transfer. There are times when an entire railcar is dropped off or picked up. This is a slow process. It requires shunting onto a siding and uncoupling the guard's van and altering the order of the cars. The train shunts back and forth numerous times until the correct order is attained. The journey to Moscow is slow. So slow that the goods train is required to park on a siding to permit a faster train to pass – an express passenger train, with light-goods wagons, carrying army personnel.

Sergei attempts to make conversation with the guard. "The potatoes in the railcars, the cargo that originated in Corrective Farm No.47, are for export. This rail line ends at Kazansky Railway Station. What happens to the railcars at that point?"

The guard interrupts his work to pour tea from a pot on the stove. He offers a mug of tea to Sergei. He resumes his tasks while sipping tea and responds to Sergei. "This train is not going to Kazansky Railway Station. It is going to the warehouse terminal in Moscow. The terminal has rail links to all other lines. As soon as the warehouse accepts this train with the goods, my responsibility ends. The warehouse administrator has the necessary bills of lading and export permits for the next stage of the journey. Your five railcars will probably join a train of 50 cars."

Sergei remembers back to when he travelled by train. He calculates that the journey from Zelenodolsk to Moscow should take 15 hours. He estimates that they have been travelling in the guard's van for over 20 hours. He asks the guard how long it will take to reach Moscow.

The guard replies, "Soon. We are almost there. Another hour or so. Don't worry. We are on schedule."

The train eventually enters Moscow. It halts at Elektrozavodskaya Station. The platform is deserted – no passengers to embark or disembark, and no goods to load or unload. A solitary soldier strides to the guard's van and enters. He speaks in a firm voice. "Sergei Falkov? Come with me!" The command is clearly directed at Sergei. The only other occupant is the guard in a railway worker's uniform.

Sergei is momentarily frozen. How did this soldier know that he is on board the train? Could the guard have communicated ahead in some way? No, the guard is not aware of his identity. He sighs in resignation. It is futile to resist. Sergei surrenders himself peacefully. He is thankful that he is not shot. But that could come later, or perhaps an extended sentence of forced labour. And this time the labour might be at the Pacific coast of Siberia where zeks dig in opencast mines. They seldom return.

Sergei is anxious. He is so worried that he pays no attention to where he is being taken. The soldier brings him to a non-descript government building – they all look alike. Sergei is ushered inside and to an office. He senses something familiar about his surroundings, not just in the uniformity of most government offices. He was here once before.

"Comrade Falkov, please take a seat."

Sergei realizes that he is standing in front of the desk of Dmitry Reshetnikov, just as he did a few months earlier. To Sergei, that seems like a long time ago – until now. Now, it feels like yesterday. Dmitry opens a desk drawer and removes a cigarette box. He invites Sergei to choose a cigarette. The nervous guest declines and regards the official's stare with trepidation. Dmitry Reshetnikov selects a cigarette, lights it and places the box back into the desk drawer. His unblinking eyes unnerve Sergei. Sergei comprehends that he is to sit.

Once Sergei is seated, the senior civil servant blinks and asks, "Comrade Falkov, do you know why you are here?"

Sergei avoids answering. He deflects it by stating, "I was brought here."

"You were brought here against your will?" Sergei declines to answer. Dmitry draws on his cigarette and makes an observation. "You look much different, Comrade Falkov, except for your American glasses. Have you changed?"

"Yes, Comrade Reshetnikov."

Dmitry asks another question. "But tell me, why do you think you are here?" He blinks at the word 'think' and resumes his steady stare.

Sergei answers, "It is my service to Mother Russia." Inwardly, he ponders, "Why is he toying with me? He has me in custody."

"Indeed. Your service to Russia." Dmitry removes a file from his drawer. He opens it and consults the pages therein. "Does your service to Russia include your inventing a 'pontoon-board'?"

Suddenly, Sergei realizes that the purpose of this meeting is to gain information on his inventions and innovations. Of course, the crafty civil servant would know of his work at the labour farm. It was recorded by the inspector. As soon as Dmitry exhausts his questions, he will surrender Sergei to his proper fate. Sergei recovers sufficiently to respond. "It is not an 'invention', Comrade Reshetnikov. It is an 'innovation'."

"How so?"

"Pontoon-boards, or a variation, were employed by the ancient Romans. I just applied the concept to the conditions in the potato fields. That is where I was labouring – the potato fields in Corrective Farm No.47."

"Yes, you are correct. Julius Caesar makes reference to them in 'De Bello Gallico'. That's 2,000 years ago." Dmitry Reshetnikov smugly displays his knowledge of Roman History.

Sergei, not wishing to be outdone, adds, "A technique he learned from the Gauls. And which he used effectively in defeating them."

Dmitry nods in agreement. "An interesting observation. One learns from his enemy and employs the enemy's techniques to defeat him."

"That's often the case. The superior force is the one that innovates – even if it means learning from his opponent." Sergei is confident that he made his point. He ceases talking.

Dmitry draws on his cigarette. He blows smoke out through the side of his mouth and asks, almost casually, "Capitalism is our enemy. Have you learned any capitalist techniques that we may use to defeat them?"

"Incentives." Sergei renders the word in English.

"Really? And have we no 'incentives' in Russia?"

"Yes. But we don't know how to market them effectively." This time Sergei uses the English word 'market'.

"You believe that we can defeat capitalism with 'marketing incentives'?"

"Perhaps not 'defeat'. I would say 'outperform'."

"'Incentives' are synonyms for 'profits'. How do you reconcile this to communism?"

"Non-monetary rewards for performance – awards, medals, honours and recognition of outstanding achievements in productivity. The quota system is often perceived as punitive. Employing incentives is a way to use a carrot rather than a stick to induce greater output – whether on the factory floor or in the farm field."

"Do away with quotas?"

"No. Rename them. 'Market' them with 'incentives'." Again, Sergei uses English words.

Dmitry stubs out his cigarette on an ashtray hidden in his desk drawer. He closes the file and places it in a lower drawer. Thus, his desk is clear. He is silent for some minutes. Sergei wonders if it was wise to speak of 'incentives' and 'marketing'. He fears that the senior civil servant may regard him as tainted by capitalism – still tainted and not rehabilitated. And what fate awaits an escaping zek? Dmitry shouts for an attendant. "Comrade Saveliev!"

Saveliev immediately enters. He must have been standing by the door in expectation of the summons. "Yes, Comrade Reshetnikov!" It is the same soldier that brought Sergei here from the train station. Only now, at the mention of the name, he recognizes him as the soldier from his previous visit to Dmitry Reshetnikov's office.

Dmitry issues an order. "Take Comrade Falkov to the colonel."

"Yes, Comrade."

Sergei braces for what is to come – execution or a forced-labour death camp.

CHAPTER FIFTEEN

In Moscow

They travel by car through Moscow. Sergei stares out through the window at the passing buildings but he doesn't see them. His mind is on his imminent meeting with the colonel. The soldier, Saveliev, is his driver and escort. They arrive at a massive brick building. There is no signage to indicate the purpose of the building, but Sergei recognizes it. He is escorted through the front doors, down a short corridor and into a room. He senses the tense atmosphere of the intimidating interior. Two stern-faced men in uniform confront him.

His soldier escort, Saveliev, speaks, "Comrade Sergei Falkov to see the colonel."

One of the stern men, a guard presumably, brings Sergei to an upper-floor office, one marked 'ADMINISTRATOR'. Once inside, Sergei stands facing a colonel sitting behind a desk. He recognizes the colonel. It is Ivan Patrushev of Corrective Labour Camps Division. The guard announces, "Comrade Sergei Falkov to see you, Comrade Colonel."

Ivan nods in acknowledgement. He gestures to the guard, who promptly exits the room. The colonel studies Sergei for a moment. Then he says, "Be seated, Comrade." Sergei sits facing him. Ivan continues.

"Sergei Falkov. It's been a few months, has it not? And look at you. I did not recognize you – shaved head, no goatee. You look Russian – except for your glasses. So, how have you been?"

Sergei answers impassively, "I've spent three months in a labour camp. You know that – Corrective Farm No.47."

"But now, you are here. Are you not?"

"Yes, Comrade Colonel."

"Tell me, how was your journey? Was it eventful?"

"I was on the train – the one with the potato cargo. You know that."

Ivan smiles. "Of course, you were on that train. We would have been upset had you **not** been on that train."

Sergei is surprised by the comment. "You were expecting me?"

"Of course. And why not? You were summoned here. The camp administrator was ordered to convey you to Moscow with the shipment of potatoes. The original date of your arrival was scheduled for the 1st of January. But the date was brought forward to coincide with the early transportation of the assigned cargo. In a way, you are four days early."

Sergei's mouth drops; his eyebrows rise. "I was summoned here?"

"Did not the camp administrator instruct you?"

"The camp administrator? He has not spoken to me – not in more than a month. And that was about the rollers I was designing for the lorries – a quick one-man device for engaging the tarpaulin covers."

This time, Ivan registers surprise. "So, who commanded you to come here?"

"No one."

"So, you just up and left, and came of your own volition?" Ivan renders this sarcastically and immediately realizes that it is literally true. He finds it amusing and laughs raucously. "What did you believe? That you were a runaway zek attempting to escape?" Ivan laughs even louder. He rises from his chair and walks around. The noise attracts the attention of the colonel's attendant who enters the office to investigate.

The concerned soldier views the laughing colonel. He inquires, "Comrade Colonel, is anything the matter?"

Ivan recovers sufficiently to respond. "Comrade, meet Sergei Falkov, an escaped zek who came to visit me." He suppresses his laughter and says, "Comrade Falkov told me an amusing story. All is in order. You may leave." The puzzled, yet relieved, soldier exits.

Ivan returns to his seat. He opens a file on his desk. He looks at Sergei and says, "Then you don't know why you are here? Where shall I start?" He shuffles through the top few pages in the file. He selects a page and refers to it. "The administrator sent us weekly reports. I must say, he was quite detailed. The inspector checked on the truth of his statements. He describes your contribution to the farm. We are pleased with your work – how you saved the crop with your innovations. And you presented other modifications to improve efficiency. This culminated in the final cargo of potatoes exceeding the original quota by 67%. That's impressive." Ivan shuffles the pages. He refers to another one. "The administrator reported that you displayed rehabilitation. That is rare in a zek after just three months of labour. Nevertheless, we examined your progress and agree. We decided that your skills should be fully employed – and more widely employed – in service to Russia. In January, you will be assigned to a position within the ministry." Ivan raises his eyes from the forms he is reading. He looks directly at

Sergei. "You have not been a zek since the 15th of December when your prisoner status was revoked. This was communicated to the camp administrator by post on the 22nd of December, with instructions to send you to Moscow with the final shipment of potatoes and report to us here. We included a letter of introduction for your use, should you be challenged."

Sergei is dumbfounded. "I didn't know any of this." He thinks of the period he was in hiding. All along, he was unaware that he was a free man.

Ivan slides the file across the desk. "Here. Look for yourself."

Sergei takes the file and begins to read, starting with the most recent page and working backwards. There is much to digest. Not only does it exhibit the innovations he introduced, but it also lists his recommendations on prison-farm coordination. He closes the file and places it back on the desk. "Comrade Colonel, a request, if I may?"

"A request?"

"Yes, with your approval. My name is Sergei Murashko Falkov."

"I know that. It's in the file."

"From now on, I wish to be known as 'Sergei Murashko'."

"Tell me why."

"You said that you did not recognize me when I entered. You also said that I am rehabilitated. Therefore, I wish to shake off any association with my former self, especially my former zek status. Sergei Falkov is dead to the world. Sergei Murashko is the new man."

"I agree, Comrade Murashko." Ivan places the file inside a desk drawer. "Your business here is done. You will now be taken to your flat in Ulitsa Bol'shaya Lubyanka. You remember it, no doubt? The street is within 15 minutes' walking distance of Red Square and the Kremlin. It is popular with the Kremlin officials who live there."

*　　*　　*　　*　　*

Sergei Murashko quickly becomes attuned to his new life. He receives a crisp new uniform, delivered to his flat. He obtains new glasses from the ministry, a pair with circular frames. In his new job at the ministry, he looks like a Russian in every respect. His first duty is to examine the relationship between the punitive nature of labour camps against the demand for productivity and

190

submit his recommendations. Sergei draws an analogy between mules and zeks. Mules as most productive when they are fed, rested and nourished. Zeks should be afforded the same treatment, not for the sake of the zek, but to maximize productivity. Lazy mules are beaten; same with zeks. Disobedient and non-productive mules are unusable and are put down. This also applies to zeks – a non-working zek is a dead zek. Incentives to higher achievement should be employed – the 'carrot-to-the-mule' approach. However, zeks are not mules. Whereas mules will always be mules, zeks are required to rehabilitate. Sergei stresses a balance between the need for punishment and attaining production quotas. Either one should not be at the expense of the other. Good productive work, in itself, ought to render rehabilitation.

The ministry is impressed with Sergei's analysis. Sergei is appointed an inspector of corrective labour camps. His assignment is to improve the efficiency and productivity of under-performing camps. He notes that this applies to 72% of camps.

*　　*　　*　　*　　*

At Corrective Farm No.47, the administrator reads the newly-arrived post of 27 December. His jaw drops when he reads the directive to have Sergei Falkov released from zek duties and have him report to the ministry for a new assignment. He is to accompany the cargo consignment to Moscow, but not later than 01 January. Denis Novak swallows. Should he respond to this directive, he wonders? A letter written today will not reach the ministry before the train arrives in Moscow with the cargo. His only option is to drive to the railway station and send a telegram. He goes to the service garage and requests the use of a lorry. The lorries are being serviced. Because of two gruelling weeks on the road, Vladimir is replacing the tires. It is another half-hour before a lorry is available. While he waits, Lieutenant Novak reads the remainder of the post. The good news is that he is considered for a promotion and is directed to report to the ministry on 05 January. Denis is anxious. The debacle with Sergei Falkov could derail his promotion.

It is 9:40 am when Denis Novak leaves the farm and drives to the railway station. The telegraph office is closed when he arrives. He waits until the following day. On the next morning, he sends the message: 'Segrei Falkov zek no more – will not arrive on train'. He intends to convey that Sergei Falkov, the zek, is dead. The ministry understands it to mean that Sergei Falkov is no longer a zek. And that he will not be on the later train, the one originally scheduled for 01 January.

They regard the message as redundant. They know that Sergei Falkov has been released from his sentence and that he has already arrived in Moscow. They disregard the telegram. Denis waits for an hour in expectation of a response or acknowledgement. When nothing arrives, he drives back to the prison camp.

On 04 January, an army lorry arrives and transports the administrator, the zeks and the remaining guards to reassignments. On 05 January, Lieutenant Denis Novak is promoted and assigned to responsible duties in the Kremlin. He is relieved that he is released from corrective labour camps. Vladimir, Pyotr, Gregori, Mikhail and Boris settle in for the winter, the sole occupants of Corrective Farm No.47. Vladimir checks on the store of potatoes, the surplus that remains behind – over two railcar-loads of potatoes. The ministry appears to be unaware of its existence. He plans to add them to the next crop harvest. It will give a head start to reaching the next potato crop quota.

CHAPTER SIXTEEN

THE CARROT AND THE STICK

1929 is another year at Corrective Farm No.47. It is late July. Vladimir Kotyakov drives the farm truck to the previous year's potato fields. This area will be harrowed in August for planting winter oats. But first, the rye harvest requires his attention. He swings around the future oat fields and proceeds to the area of current activity – the rye fields.

He reflects on the recent changes. In January, he was promoted to senior administrator of the corrective labour farm. The prison has a new junior administrator subordinate to Vladimir. Consequently, Vladimir has authority over the entire facility – the corrective prison plus the farm. Upon assuming his new position, he has made a few, but significant, changes to the operation. To a large extent, the farm is now self-sufficient in food. Potatoes, beets and cabbages are grown for their local consumption. Ducks and geese provide eggs and occasional meat. The new flock of chickens is a welcome source of food. And two dairy cows supply milk and butter. He achieved this by entering into a close working relationship with the neighbouring collective farm. This would not have happened under the previous administration where the emphasis was on zek correction and rehabilitation. Today, the focus is on crop production. And the farm manager determines how it is executed. The correctional facility supplies labour to the farm but does not interfere with farming policies. Whereas the farm has undergone significant changes, the zeks are not treated any differently or any better than before, except for the improved quality of their diet.

The Chuvashia Republic is also changing. It is modernizing at a rapid rate. Electricity is installed in the capital of Kanash and is being extended to the rest of the region. A railroad runs through the capital. And recently, a new station for goods transit was constructed. When Vladimir next needs to bring a loaded lorry to the railway, he will drive two hours south instead of nine hours north.

Either because of, or despite, the close working relationship between the corrective labour farm and the collective farm, Gregori and Olga married in May. This would have been problematic a year ago. There is a strict rule that prohibits the presence of women in corrective labour camps. Normally, it would be impossible for Gregori to accommodate a wife on the corrective farm. And conversely, Gregori would not be permitted to live outside the facility. Today, however, due to the inter-relationship of the two farms, Gregori has reason to spend time on the collective farm and

Olga is required to spend time on the corrective labour farm. And if this is often in overnight stays, no one objects.

Vladimir reaches the rye fields. He observes the zeks at work wielding sickles. The current allotment of zek labourers is 98. The zek labourers are clumsy and slow. They lack the skills of experienced farm labourers. Short-statured workers, of 150cms or less, wield sickles with greater dexterity and efficiency. Peasant workers, including women and children, are especially skilled at this task. The zeks, working with backs bent, slice at the wrong angle. The short-cut stalks are difficult to assemble into sheaves suitable for stooks. And unstable stooks are liable to collapse or be blown over. And if the grains are close to the ground, they fail to dry sufficiently for threshing. Furthermore, they are an invitation to vermin at ground level. In damp conditions, rye is highly susceptible to the ergot fungus. Consumption of infected rye by humans and animals results in a serious medical condition known as ergotism.

Vladimir berates the guards for permitting slow shoddy work. He orders them to beat the zeks into line. If he is to harvest the grain successfully, he requires the work to be executed fast and efficiently. The zeks respond to the beatings. Many of them achieve a passable degree of proficiency. One or two respond favourably and execute their tasks adroitly. Others are dismal failures. If Vladimir is to succeed in saving the harvest, he needs experienced workers from the collective farm. He orders the guards to have the zeks work two hours extra. Then, he drives to the collective farm and meets with Olga. He obtains actual workers from her, sufficiently skilled for reaping.

That night, Vladimir writes a report. He gives an account of the poor quality of the zek labour and explains that he relies on the neighbouring collective farm to provide skilled labour to save the rye harvest. On the following morning, he witnesses a team of farmworkers arrive under the supervision of Olga. He puts her in charge of the work detail. Thereupon, he drives to Kanash and posts his report to the ministry.

The rye sheaves are adequately stooked within a few days. Thereafter, the zeks are transported by lorry to the collective farm where they toil daily at harvesting beet. This requires little skill but lots of drudging in the dirt. Having zeks harvest the collective's beets, accomplishes the quid pro quo of inter-farm cooperation. When the beet harvest is collected, the zeks are employed once more back in the corrective labour farm, this time in threshing the rye. The resulting grain is packed into sacks and stored in dry airy stalls in the barn. The resulting straw is bailed and stored in the upper lofts. Vladimir is relieved that he reached the required quota for rye. Without the support of the collective farmworkers, he would have been woefully short of the target. He files his report. He waits for instructions to deliver the rye crop to the grain depot in Kanash.

The farm administrator's next task is to prepare last year's potato fields for planting winter oats. Oats planted in September will hibernate in a dormant state over the winter and be harvested in the following July or August. The zeks are put to work in the former potato fields. They employ spades to turn the earth and break the soil. Afterwards, they drag harrows of heavy frames with teeth to break up clods and remove weeds. Vladimir is pleased that the work is on schedule. After sowing the oats, a process that he entrusts solely to his farm staff, the zeks will haul the harrows once more to cover the seeds.

On a day when the zeks are active in digging and harrowing under the strict supervision of the guards, an unexpected car arrives at the corrective labour farm. The driver identifies himself to the guard at the gate, who waves him through. The car comes to a halt at the entrance to the prison building. The occupant exits the car and strides decisively to the door. This is an inspector from the ministry on a surprise visit to the labour camp. He demands to see the administrator. The guard escorts him to the prison administrator's office, the room once occupied by Denis Novak and currently occupied by the prison administrator.

The guard introduces the newcomer to the administrator. "Comrade Sergei Murashko to see you, Comrade Administrator. He is an inspector from the ministry."

The prison administrator is taken by surprise. He is in the process of assessing the zeks' performance when he is interrupted. From the uniform and demeanour of the visitor, he deduces that this is a person of high authority. He shuts the register and stands to attention. He straightens his jacket and salutes. "Welcome Comrade Inspector. Please have a seat." He gestures to the guest chair. "I am Konstantin Kobylkin, senior guard and administrator of the corrective facility. How may I be of assistance?"

Sergei remains standing. He looks coldly at him and says, "You are the prison administrator. I wish to see Comrade Vladimir Kotyakov, the senior administrator of the corrective labour farm. Is this not his office?"

"Comrade Kotyakov prefers to use the office in the

service garage. He says that it is closer to the heart of the operation. This office is…"

"Take me to him."

"At once, Comrade Inspector."

A very nervous Konstantin escorts the inspector to the service garage. Vladimir is not present when they arrive, and the office door is locked. The prison administrator apologizes and instructs a guard to locate the farm manager. Konstantin is unsure of what to say. He plays safe and keeps silent. Sergei, on the other hand, pokes about in the garage, looking hither and thither into the gloomy bays and recesses of the vast building. He hesitates at the stove. He examines the contents of a pot simmering on the surface. He casually removes a mug from an adjacent hook and pours some of the hot liquid into it. He tastes the liquid and says, "Potato tea." He consumes the tea in a single swig. At this point, Vladimir enters the garage. Sergei looks at him and places the empty mug at the back of the stove behind the pot.

Vladimir speaks. "Comrade Inspector, I did not know you were here. Forgive me. I was at the barn checking on the stored rye."

"Good. I'm interested in the rye. Take me there."

Vladimir, Konstantin and Sergei stride to the barn. Vladimir identifies the sacks of grain. They are stacked inside wooden cubicles. Vladimir conducts a tour of the barn. "See here, Comrade Inspector, the rye is stored in a dry airy environment. The quota is reached – of course, you know that from the reports. And we await instructions to ship the crop to the grain depot in Kanash." Vladimir makes no mention of the potatoes stored in the upper loft – the equivalent of two loaded railcars. These are his cushion for the next potato harvest when the quota is expected to be greater than the previous year's total.

Sergei prods a bag with a finger and nods in approval. "I am pleased with the harvested crop. However, I am **not** pleased with the zeks. You reported that the quality of their work was lacking."

"That is correct. I reported that the zeks were insufficiently skilled at wielding sickles. The way they hacked at the stalks was damaging to the crop, resulting in uneven sheaves that could not be stooked securely. And worse, they were unable to maintain the required work output."

Sergei turns to the senior guard and asks, "Is this true,

Comrade? That the zeks are lazy?"

"Comrade Inspector, we beat them, but they are clumsy and stupid. Only a few perform well. I have a record of their daily performances. I can show you which zeks excel and which ones fall short of their daily work quotas."

"Of course, you have a record. You are required to monitor each zek's progress to assess his improvement to rehabilitation. That's your job. Now show me your daily work register for the period in question."

Konstantin departs to fetch his register. Meanwhile, Vladimir explains that he saved the rye harvest by obtaining labourers from the collective farm in Bichurga-Baishevo. And that, in the spirit of cooperation, he later transferred the zeks to the collective farm to assist with their beet harvest. The inspector nods but does not comment. He is interrupted by the return of the prison administrator.

The administrator waves the register above his head and shouts, "The register, Comrade Inspector. I have it here."

Sergei takes the register. "Good. Now take me to the zeks. I will demonstrate how motivation is instilled in them."

Vladimir interjects. "The zeks are at work, digging and harrowing. They are five kilometres away by the river."

"Do you not have a farm truck?" Sergei asks this while eyeing the farm truck parked close by.

Vladimir suppresses a smile. "If you are prepared to travel by farm truck, I can bring you to the work fields."

Sergei gestures to the two men. "Then, let's go."

Vladimir drives the truck across the fields. Sergei sits in the passenger seat flipping through the register; the guard rides in the truck bed. The ground under the truck is firm. The wheels disturb the dusty surface as it bumps along at 30kph. They reach the fields in ten minutes. The three men exit the truck and view the zeks at work. Most of the zeks are digging into the ground that previously contained the potato crop. They turn the surface sod and whack it to break it into clods. As they progress, other zeks drag harrows to break the clods and render the soil fine enough for oat seeding. Where the teeth of the harrows snag objectionable weeds, the zeks gather them for burning.

Sergei directs the guards to assemble the zeks by the

riverbank. He issues specific instructions to the prison administrator to have the guards prepared for his orders. When the zeks are gathered to Sergei's approval, he addresses them from the ridge. "Comrades, you toil here in honourable work. The fruits of your labour benefit Mother Russia." His voice carries from the ridge down to the riverbank. He continues. "You, the labourers, also benefit from the work. It is a step towards your eventual rehabilitation." He waits for the message to sink in. "Here, at this labour camp, you are generously fed – a portion of fish or meat every day; you have a dry bed at night; you have stout clothing. You are better off than most of your comrades living and working on collective farms. And, in return, you are asked to do one simple thing – fulfill your daily work quota."

The zeks stand stoically in line. It is a propaganda speech. They are not impressed. But they endure it without any display of emotion. Sergei consults the work register. He delivers a stroke that captures the attention of the fatigued workers. He calls out one zek. "Prisoner number 1407! Step forward!"

A startled zek steps forward one pace.

Sergei resumes speaking. "Prisoner number 1407, I do not address you by name. Your name will return to you when you are rehabilitated. At that time, you will be a person again. Now hear this. The work log reveals that you consistently perform above your assigned quota. As a reward, your sentence is herewith reduced by six months."

As this announcement registers with them, a silence falls perceptively over the assembled zeks, followed by an audible shuffling of feet. Sergei continues. "This register details your performance. Other prisoners are recognized for their work. This does not go unnoticed. Good workers are recognized. They earn favourable comments that will be considered in their rehabilitation and early release." Sergei hesitates. He sees that the zeks are attentive to what he imparts. He delivers another unexpected stroke. "Alas, some prisoners fall short of their work quotas." He addresses his following comments to the under-performers. "You have critical remarks recorded against you in the register – 'failure to meet daily quotas'. And what is the result? Your sentences will be extended." At this point, he raises his voice. "Prisoners 1222, 1389, 1401! Step back one pace! The rest of you, stand up here on the ridge."

A minute later, the summoned zeks stand on the ridge. They are directed to observe the three lone zeks at the river's edge. Sergei resumes speaking. "These three prisoners have consistently failed to meet their target."

The three zeks appear apprehensive. One is tall and stooped. He is obviously frail. The second zek is disabled by an injured knee. He is unable to bend that leg, hence he has trouble walking and he has difficulty performing the required tasks. The third zek is clearly dazed and is unable to grasp what is occurring. He smiles nervously and darts his eyes left and right. Sergei resumes speaking, "Abject failure results in termination of the sentence. Guards, deal with them!"

Three guards descend the ridge, draw their sidearms and shoot the three zeks in their heads. Three bodies fall back into the flowing water and are sucked out into the current of the river. Sergei announces, "Back to work!" and the shocked zeks return to digging and harrowing. He returns the register to the prison administrator and says, "The carrot is preferable to the stick. But if the carrot does not work…" He re-enters the truck and gestures to Vladimir to return to the farm. Not another word is spoken until he reaches his car. As he enters, the inspector imparts a closing remark to the prison administrator and the farm manager. "You will hear from me. Meanwhile, keep me informed." He drives off in a cloud of dust.

A short time later, Vladimir returns to the service garage. He is pensive as he ponders the recent occurrence. He throws another log onto the fire to heat the stove. He watches the wood ignite and spark. It burns quickly. By morning the embers will be cold. The mug is still on the stove. He rinses it with clean water. As he peers into the flickering flame, he remembers that for a while the stove remained hot overnight. Back in December, from the time Sergei Falkov disappeared to the day of the final delivery of potatoes to the railcars, he was able to reignite the fire in the morning from the hot overnight coals. That was also the last time he noticed drops of water in the bent mug – until now. He hangs the bent mug on its hook and mutters, "What **really** happened to Sergei Falkov?"

Acknowledgements:

Britannica.com – information on forced-labour camps

Russian Federation website – statistics on crop production and transportation

Us Conductors by Sean Michaels – where I got the idea for an inventor incarcerated in a Russian labour camp

Wikipedia.com – history of the Russian government during the Stalin era

ABOUT THE AUTHOR

Fergus Patrick Egan was born in 1945 in Donegal in the northwest of Ireland. He spent 20 years in retail banking, including 10 years in Toronto, Canada. Over the course of 30 years, he worked in the Canadian travel industry. He currently resides in Ontario, Canada.

Other books by the author:

Black Donnelly, Rats and Pigs

The Coin and the Key

The Famine Field

Dorinda Trapper of Red Rapids

Lanta: A Song of the Sea